THE DUBIOUS SALVATION OF JACK V.

Jacques Strauss is a thirty-three-year-old South African. He studied philosophy at university, obsessed over Derrida and now writes reams of corporate copy for a London firm.

D1348069

JACQUES STRAUSS

The Dubious Salvation of Jack V.

VINTAGE BOOKS
London

Published by Vintage 2012

2 4 6 8 10 9 7 5 3 1

First published in Great Britain in 2011 by
Jonathan Cape

Vintage
Random House, 20 Vauxhall Bridge Road,
London SW1V 2SA

www.vintage-books.co.uk

Addresses for companies within The Random House Group Limited
can be found at: www.randomhouse.co.uk/offices.htm

The Random House Group Limited Reg. No. 954009

A CIP catalogue record for this book
is available from the British Library

ISBN 9780099555070

The Random House Group Limited supports The Forest Stewardship
Council (FSC®), the leading international forest certification
organisation. Our books carrying the FSC label are printed on FSC®
certified paper. FSC is the only forest certification scheme endorsed
by the leading environmental organisations, including Greenpeace.
Our paper procurement policy can be found at:
www.randomhouse.co.uk/environment

Printed and bound by CPI Group (UK) Ltd, Croydon, CR0 4YY

For my parents

And instead of just goodness and greatness
There have burst through the tar, from the tar of the street
royally red and white
mottled mushrooms
what is awesome and what is simple
and evil and simple
and simple and humble
out through the crack that is you
The earth is not singular

'As a child,' N.P. van Wyk Louw
Translated by Adam Small

PROLOGUE

The booby-trapped universe

WHEN I WAS eleven I was too old to cry in front of my friends, but not too old to fake a stomach ache at a sleep-over if I was suddenly overcome with homesickness, because my friend's mother had made mutton stew and prayed before the meal and bought no-name-brand toothpaste that tasted funny. When I was eleven I had a nightmare and went to my parents' room and interrupted them having sex. I was old enough to know what they were doing, but I did not pretend I was half asleep because it was that horrible nightmare about the dead children with the stitched-up lips and the stitched-up eyes, who came out of the black lake to chase me.

When I was eleven I was old enough to join the scholar patrol, which meant I could stop traffic with my stop sign on a stick so that the children in grade one could cross the road, but I did not understand that the child who got hit by a bus was dead forever and ever and that this was monumental and that it could happen to me.

When I was eleven I began to realise that my parents

I

didn't always like my friends' parents and that it was possible for my friends' parents to dress in the wrong way and say the wrong things. It was possible for them to be common, crass or snobs. I considered my parents' judgement perfect and did not question anything they did or said or believed. But by the time I was eleven, I had developed tact; I did not say, 'My mother thinks your mother is vulgar.'

When I was eleven I was stupid enough to try to have sex with a shampoo bottle. And when it got stuck and I panicked, I was old enough to know that if my mother saw this, she would know, she would just know, what I had been doing. But I called for her anyway and she said, 'If you calm down, it will come off by itself.'

When I was eleven I was too old to bathe with my little sister, mainly because I was at that age where I tried foolish things, like violating the toiletries. I was old enough to know that peeing in the bath was disgusting but young enough not to care and do it anyway because I was too lazy to get out of the tepid water. When I was eleven I no longer had to eat mangoes in the bath. I was old enough not to spill the corrosive juices all over myself, and have to be rinsed off after eating them. This was good, because only I knew what I still did in there.

When I was eleven I was too scared to go into the local store that always smelt of incense and was run by the local Indian woman, where the teenage boys went to have their ears pierced, because it was dark and gloomy and the Indian lady was bad-tempered. Mothers worried about their sons getting hepatitis from those filthy *koelies*. This I understood. But I did not know that fathers were more concerned about what it meant when they discovered their sons wanted earrings.

I was frightened too of the local prosthetist and would

cross the road to avoid his shop. I did not know that running a high-street store full of prosthetic limbs, artfully arranged in the window, was unusual and that not every suburb had a shop like this, sandwiched between the baker and the grocer.

When I was eleven my Afrikaans was still almost as good as my English but I could never remember anything from Zulu class other than how to say Hello; What is your name?; My name is Jack; What is your surname?; My surname is Viljee; Where do you work?; I work in Johannesburg; meat; milk; spoon; train; machine; fork.

When I was eleven I was old enough to know that some of my friends' parents voted for the Democratic Party, a few for the Conservative Party, but most for the National Party. I was old enough to know these things mattered but that it was best not to talk about it. I knew that Margaret Thatcher was not the same as the Queen, but I didn't understand the difference.

When I was eleven I no longer had health class at school and did general science instead, which was good because health was for babies and taught you about stupid things like washing your hands after using the bathroom. Even though we often didn't, it wasn't like we needed to be told that this was what you were *supposed* to do. And when I was eleven I learnt to do fancy colouring with pencil shavings and fringed the maps of Africa with cobalt blue to show that this was where the sea started.

When I was eleven I started using the words 'damn', 'shit' and 'hell' in front of my friends, though none of us managed the word 'fuck' because it was too rude and we would be so startled by that syllable issuing from our young mouths that we would be rendered speechless.

3

When I was eleven I learnt that people didn't only have sex when they wanted babies, they did it for fun too. When I asked my mother how it was possible to have sex for fun if you didn't want a baby, she said mysteriously, 'There are ways.' When I was younger I'd been told that making babies had something to do with a man going to the toilet followed by a woman. For a long time it puzzled me and I observed my parents' habits carefully, but never once was there anything resembling a baby in the toilet.

When I was eleven I wanted to be a pilot because I thought it was the most magnificent profession in the world, even though I'd only ever been on an aeroplane once, flying from Johannesburg to Durban. When we took family or friends to the airport and they boarded a jumbo jet it made me want to cry with jealousy, for they seemed indifferent to these machines which I thought were so beautiful that they approached holiness.

When I was eleven I realised that I would never be good at cricket or soccer, so I decided rugby was best, because what I lacked in skill I could make up for with brute force. People said soccer was for ruffians and rugby was for gentlemen, but deep down I wanted to be good at cricket. I wanted to bat with Chad in the A team who was handsome and an orphan and lived in Mayfair Boys' Home. When I was eleven I thought it was very romantic to be an orphan, though only for a short while because I couldn't really manage without my parents.

When I was eleven I had nightmares about executions because I'd seen a film in which a woman was gassed and a television programme in which they strapped a man into an electric chair. I was glad they only hanged people in South Africa because this was less gruesome. In Spain they strangled you but the proper word was *garrotte* – so you would say, 'In Spain they garrotte people. If you kill someone you will be garrotted.' In China they shot you and in America they had lots of ways to kill people but their favourites were the electric chair and the lethal injection. In France they used to cut off your head with a guillotine, but they didn't do this any more, which was good, because this was the most terrible of all.

When I was eleven I believed in the Loch Ness Monster, the Yeti, God and Jesus and his disciples and the crucifixion and Adam and Eve and evolution, and when people disputed Darwin I pointed out that the coelacanth had been found right here in South Africa, under their very noses, which proved, *proved* we were descended from monkeys (though I wasn't sure how). And if people asked how a fish proved *anything* I said that if they needed it explained they would never understand, and left it at that.

When I was eleven I realised the gardener's cigarettes smelt funny because they were made of dagga, but I did not know you could buy it at most petrol stations. I thought all drugs were instantly addictive and if you took LSD, the worst drug of all, you would go mad and there was nothing anyone could do for you. If you took LSD you'd have to live on the streets and your mother would have to disown you. When she walked past you she'd have to say, 'I don't know who he is.' That's why when we were eleven our teachers didn't have to warn us about taking drugs. We knew. The only drug that was fine was dagga because black people could smoke it all day long without any ill effects.

When I was eleven I would masturbate everywhere because I thought nobody could possibly know what I was doing.

When I was eleven I didn't know that it was the last time I could lose myself completely in games of the imagination, where something was what it was by virtue of the fact that I said, 'This thing is such-and-such, and that thing is such-and-such. OK? Let's play.'

When I was eleven I betrayed Susie, our housekeeper, my friend, my second mother, and perhaps in other significant ways, my first. My betrayal was childish but nevertheless devastating, though of course I could not have known this at the time. Does one hold an eleven-year-old responsible for these things? Does one forgive them these things because half baked, half formed, they're still clumsy; fumbling in a world that is more dangerous to them and others than they could possibly appreciate? But how could I not appreciate the danger? Did I not live in a world where sitting snugly between the baker and the greengrocer, for all to see, was a prosthetist? Did I not realise that the universe was perfectly happy to tear people's limbs off and worse also? Did I not live in a world where people were gassed and electrocuted and hanged and decapitated? Perhaps there was just something rotten at my core. I don't know what use there is in atonement, but the question is academic, for Susie is gone, which is why I will always think back to the time I was eleven; a memory vomit of friendships and forgiveness but most of all betrayal, all of a minor kind, but dear to me, of course, it being my soul and my salvation.

1

The Boers and the blacks of Linden Extension

MY FAMILY LIVED in a very nice house, in a very nice street in the northern suburbs of Johannesburg. It would be easy to get carried away about how *nice* it all was. If one isn't careful one might easily sound nostalgic. During the hot afternoons the maids and gardeners sat beneath the trees, chatting in their native tongues. Some had babies strapped to their backs with blankets. The child would lean its head against its mother and doze while she drank a mug of tea or ate mealie meal piled on a plastic plate. Most families in Linden had maids and most of the maids lived in small rooms or cottages built in the backyard. 'A dishwashing machine,' a housewife might say, 'what would I need with one of those? All you need is a little black magic.'

The dispositions of the maids were as varied as the families they worked for. There were fat Xhosa maids who laughed easily and chatted throughout the day with their friends across six-foot walls. There were skinny Zulu maids, who regarded the Xhosas with suspicion, befriended the Ndebele women and were strict with their spoilt white charges. There were Sotho maids and Venda maids, Tswana maids and Tsonga maids. One by one they disappeared behind high walls and high gates to finish the ironing, make sandwiches for the children returning from school and start preparing the evening meal.

Of course I don't mean to suggest that the whole of Johannesburg was nice. It was the northern suburbs, a semicircular fringe around the city, that were so very nice. The best areas were those that were close to the city centre, but not within a drunken stroll of it. The southern suburbs, which completed the circle south of the city, were not very nice at all. They were poor and rough. Least nice, surrounding Johannesburg, were the giant townships where the blacks lived.

In the mapping of the degree and spread of niceness across Johannesburg, one cannot omit seedy Hillbrow in the city centre, which offered a small glimpse of what an African city could be. There was a famous record shop that sold banned albums and a famous bookshop that sold banned books. There were prostitutes there too and rent boys. Best of all was Fontana, the greatest food shop in the world. Some enterprising man had created a little of what makes America the most miraculous, wonderful place on earth, for this was the only store open seven days a week, twenty-four hours a day, and served to reassure the good citizens of Johannesburg that should they, at three o'clock on a Wednesday morning, develop an insatiable desire for a chocolate eclair, there was one place, even in dull provincial South Africa, they could go, because even in dull provincial South Africa we needed a sense of possibility. My father used to torture us late at night by saying, 'We could drive to Fontana and buy a chocolate eclair,' before sinking back into his chair. The journey into the centre of town at this late hour was as ludicrous to contemplate as a trip across the Atlantic.

The only things that seemed ominous in the northern suburbs of Johannesburg were the violent thunderstorms. Anyone who spent a summer there learnt to recognise the sudden and oppressive heat which brought about a drowsy listlessness, before the earth darkened and it rained, so heavily, so hard, that brown rivulets formed in the streets as the storm-water drains overflowed. The rainwater soaked our uniforms and school books and school bags. It was glorious to be walking down the street, as if you had jumped into a swimming pool, because it didn't matter. Within minutes it would be cool and bright and soon the school fields and pavements would be dry. Everything seemed mild and temperate and comfortable. There was an easy rhythm to the comings and goings of our families who had long grown accustomed to a wealth, which, neither spectacular nor extravagant, was sufficient for a comfortable existence replete with bicycles for younger children and cars for older, swimming pools and the occasional tennis court.

On Saturday evenings, friends and families gathered around the braai while we did cartwheels and handstands in the pool, before huddling before the open fire with towels draped around our shoulders, picking at the sizzling meat and stuffing handfuls of crisps into our mouths. Then we returned to the dark water illuminated by a submerged light, ignoring our mothers' pleas not to swim on a full stomach. Our cries and laughter, the splashing and giggling, the smell of meat, the sudden guffaw of adults, might rise up from one property and mingle with the smells and sounds of the houses further down the road, giving each weekend a celebratory air, the anaesthesia of a comfort there for the taking; and though our parents talked about the civil war – 'It will happen,' they said, 'it is inevitable' – I'm not so sure they ever really believed it, as if by recognising a thing, by naming it, their prescience would dispel its possibility. And so eleven-year-olds didn't really believe it either and there was little to dispel the general niceness of it all.

I was not, as a child, entirely satisfied with the composition of my family. I had an English mother and an Afrikaans father. It would have been simpler, I thought, to be one thing or the other, so that when my English friends said something mean about Afrikaners I could join in without feeling guilty and without feeling shame that I was doing it for all the wrong reasons. Similarly in the company of hardened Afrikaners, I would not have to convince them that I was as much a Boer as any of them, that my blood was not tainted by a trace of those English poofdas.

Also, I thought it unfortunate that I had two sisters. One would have been tolerable, but *two* was an extravagance on my mother's part. I arrived in the world with a sister in place who assumed – for she had an imperious nature – her seniority and superiority in all matters. Older brothers were glamorous, far more capable of inducting me into the world of men than my haughty sister Lisa. As I watched my mother's belly swell month by month I thought the whole situation might be rectified with the arrival of a younger brother. The only thing better than having an object of veneration was *being* an object of veneration. I could be the inductor rather than the inductee. As things stood, I was a loss to the world of brotherhood. By the age of nine I had discovered masturbation without the aid of any instruction; none of my friends had – a fact I confirmed with them in adolescence when these things were more freely spoken about – even Aaron, to whom arbitrary nature had gifted a generously proportioned man dick, only started jacking off at fourteen and then only when we told him what to do, told him to persist, 'until something happens, Aaron'. After that he progressed quickly and was soon proselytising the joy of sticking your thumb up your arse – a regular little Jack Horner – but still. This proved, surely, that I was instinctively primed to lead in the way of masculinity. Older brothers intuited the necessary information and passed it on. I knew I would make a very a superior sort of older brother. I mean superior to *other* older brothers, not necessarily superior to my imaginary sibling – for in my mind, brothers were simply younger or older versions of myself. Perfect, I thought, in every way. So Rachel's arrival in the world was a blow. Rachel was imperfect in almost every way. I even checked again when my mother brought her home, in case she'd been mistaken; perhaps the crucial appendage had become lodged in her not inconsiderable rolls of fat; perhaps it was inverted and would, much to everyone's relief, eventually pop out.

My older sister Lisa had a horsy-faced friend called Nicola, who slapped me around quite a lot – she was mean because she had an ugly birthmark on the side of her face from which sprouted coarse black hairs, and because her parents were alcoholics in the hysterical sense (English alcoholics), which meant a lot of screaming and shouting and bad behaviour and divorce. And my younger sister had a posh little friend called Julia – pronounced Joo-leee-aah – who said 'couch' instead of settee, as in 'Come he-re and sit on the cow-ch', and lived in Westcliffe towards which all the old money gravitated as opposed to Sandton which was for the Jews. Not all the Jews of course; the kugels mainly and their bagel husbands. The moderate Jews lived in Greenside and the real Jews, the Orthodox ones, the-ringlets-and-hats-and-not-switching-on-lights-on-the-Sabbath Jews, lived in Yeoville and marched in mournful procession to synagogue.

Julia's arrival caused some consternation in the Viljee household because she used words that my mother, inexplicably, did not approve of. For instance, when Julia asked to use the *loo*, my sister reported the matter to my mother who had to perform a prompt about-face to conceal her irrational abhorrence for the word. 'Don't be so silly. There is nothing wrong with the word *loo*,' she said to my bemused younger sister. There were a great many words my mother disapproved of. People did pees and poos in toilets. They most certainly did not do number ones or twos in the lav or the WC. A person might be excused for making a bripsy, but never a fart. Boys had penises and girls had vaginas. Both boys and girls had bottoms. Only people who lived in Brixton or Mayfair had fannies, *piels*, butts, bums, *totties* or arses.

I guess around eleven we all thought that to coax our dicks out of hibernation we should stop calling them 'willies' and start referring to them as 'cocks', but my mother detested this word almost as much as the Afrikaans equivalent, *voël*, which means 'bird'. Calling your cock a *voël* was a very Afrikaans and manly thing to do. It was enough to make my willy look bigger and my voice sound deeper. The odd thing about my mother's aversion to certain innocuous words is that my father had a filthy mouth. His favourite words were 'fuck-face' and 'cunt'. Prolonged exposure to my father's foul language led my younger sister to coin the insult 'vagina-face'. Etymologically and biologically speaking we thought this a good insult; good insults should make reference to the sexual organs and surely nothing could be as bad has having a face that looked like a vagina.

Blaspheming was absolutely *verboten*. Nobody ever said 'God' or 'God damn' unless somebody died, in which case you were permitted to say 'Oh my God' but not of course 'God damn' and then only if the death was unexpected; and the only thing worse than saying 'Jesus' or 'Christ' was saying them in combination. Even the corrupted forms were frowned upon. For instance, *'jissie'* was considered unacceptable by my family. The only word not offensive from a religious point of view was *'jislaaik'*, but it was considered unsophisticated (as in *'Jislaaik*, this thing is expensive, hey!')and vulgar (as in *'Jislaaik*, she has big tits'). Even though I grew up in a family of atheists I never used the words 'God' or 'Jesus' or 'Jesus Christ' and certainly not 'Jesus fucking Christ'.

It was accepted in my family that Rachel, my younger sister, was my father's favourite and both my siblings maintained that I was my mother's favourite, which was possibly true. But my mother's preference for me (if this was so, of which I am not fully convinced) was a lesser betrayal for she had only one son and mothers are supposed to prefer their sons. Not that I think my older sister minded. She knew that she was the most wilful and the most difficult. People said my older sister could be very prickly. Even my parents said that: 'Your sister can be very prickly' – a quality she inherited from our father. She had a habit of saying certain penetrating things that others thought best left unsaid. They were not merely tactless things; there is no skill in saying what is *merely* tactless. They were things that everyone had a vague sense of, that flittered on the periphery of the consciousness, but had not quite shaped into a clear thought until they found a willing medium in the mouth of my sister, the family oracle.

Sometimes we forgot that my sister had feelings. Once, when she came back from the hairdresser with a bad perm, I laughed and said to her, 'You look like a poodle.' She started crying and ran to her room. I felt bad because I knew my sister didn't have many friends. My parents sometimes tried to talk to her about this. They said, 'Lisa, sometimes you can be very strident.' Those were the two words for my sister: 'strident' and 'prickly'. I didn't know what strident meant and assumed it had something to do with the way she walked. Rachel and I knew that Lisa had a harder time than us growing up. My parents were poor when Lisa was born so she didn't have many toys and they lived in a house without an indoor toilet. And when she was young she was a bit fat and was teased at school. Her favourite activity in the world was Brownies. She was, if you were to look at the photographs, the proudest and most devoted Brownie that ever there was, but when my parents moved she had to leave the Brownies behind. Sometimes when she got home from her not very nice school, she would change into her Brownie uniform and make cookies with Susie which was just about the saddest thing I ever saw. Whenever I thought about my sister, trying to recreate her Brownie group because she didn't have many friends and because the people at school called her 'fatty', I felt bad about the mean things I said to her, especially the day I said she looked like a poodle because one tended to forget that even though she wasn't fat any more, even though she was strident and prickly, she was sensitive too.

In the year I turned eleven my sister went off to university to earn her degree, returning at weekends to tell me about the Milgram experiment and show me Rorschach cards. 'Don't ever say, I just see a black mass,' she advised, 'it reveals pathological tendencies,' or 'You're far too in thrall to authority figures, Jack. You'd make a good Nazi though. Maybe you should join the army.'

My younger sister was focusing all her energies on being adorable – at which she was remarkably successful. She was achingly adorable. I understood that expression used by adults: 'You're so cute, I could just eat you up.' She was like a fat, chocolate-covered doughnut and our affection manifested itself in cannibalistic longing. I would not have been surprised if my mother served roast baby sister for Christmas lunch. She became a first-class swimmer and went on to graduate in law. Lisa and I later agreed that the twenty-one-year streak of adorableness wore thin, but when I was eleven my sister was only six and this impressive trajectory was not yet evident. We regarded her as sweet, but dim. With any luck, we thought, she had inherited all the family's fat genes and our propensity to slight chunkiness could find full expression in just one obese sibling.

My parents stopped with my younger sister; this was as many children as they could decently have had. Any more and we would have begun to resemble Afrikaners or white trash (I don't think anyone would ever have mistaken us for Catholics. Only the Portuguese and the Lebanese were Catholics). My older sister was schooled entirely in Afrikaans, my younger sister entirely in English. If you were to put us in a line, most Afrikaans at one end and most English at the other, my mother and Rachel would be the English pole, my father and Lisa the Afrikaans pole, and I would be dead centre, aligning myself with whomever I preferred at any given time.

Susie Mafisa had worked for my family since I was born. She was a large woman with ample breasts. Her skin was dark, but not so dark that you might think she originally came from northern Africa. She wore baby-blue or mint-green overalls bought from the OK Bazaar on Seventh Street. She covered her head with a *kopdoek*, a headscarf, which together with the apron was included in the Domestic's Pack. Instead of putting the soles of her feet into her faded grey *tekkies*, she stood on top of them, crushing the fabric of the sneaker to reveal the pink-brown soles of her feet. Susie had rigid opinions on almost every matter, which she shared with me while doing the ironing as I ate my sandwiches after school.

'The Zulus are very dangerous people. Sophie, she's a nice Zulu, but the Zulus have a big temper, even Sophie, she has a big temper. That is why the Zulus are always fighting. You must watch out for them. But Sophie, she is nice.'(Sophie worked for our next-door neighbours. They had four sons, aged ten to eighteen, who all lived in a large room laid out like a dormitory, with a bed and desk for each child. I wasn't friends with them, though I was jealous of the youngest because he had *three* older brothers.) Susie sipped her tea and said, 'The Zulus are like the Boers, very dangerous. Your uncles and your aunties, they are real Boers – am I right? That time they come here I see them. They look and they see me. They see I call your daddy by his name. They think, this *ousie*, she's very cheeky. Am I right? Your granny she say to me – Jack, I laugh when I think this – she say to me, "Susie, if you were working for me, you would call me Madam." Ha ha! But I like your granny. I like Ouma so much.'

She filled the iron and reached for another shirt.

'I never see Ouma any more. You must tell her I pray for her. On Sunday, I give fifty cents the church must pray for her. You see, she will get better. Jack! You mustn't leave your glass there. I will hit you. Wha! Wha!' She threw her head back and laughed. Susie's mind was, in certain respects, peculiar. There was something unnerving to the swings, not in mood, but tone. I can only imagine that she foresaw an avalanche of mess should she stop even for a moment the monitoring of the household's cleanliness, so that while one part of her brain was commiserating with your dead or dying granny, another was on the constant lookout for stray crumbs, dirty dishes and wet towels.

'You are so naughty you! But I love you – you are my baby. *Shaya wena*, Jack! You know this? *Shaya wena* – it's Zulu – it means I will hit you. Wha! Wha!'

She also believed violence, of the non-disfiguring variety, was a healthy and unambivalent form of affection, hence the not infrequent expression, 'I love you so much. I will hit you.'

When Susie was really angry she would invoke Matthew – the son of her former employer. '*Matt* he love me,' she would say. 'Matt was a nice nice boy – so nice. Not like you. Matt he never make mess. Matt was such a handsome boy. Every day he come to me and say, "I love you, Mama Susie." Not like you and your sisters. You don't love me. If you love me you wouldn't make a mess. I tell your daddy – you and your sisters are so spoilt. I wish you were like Matthew.'

I loathed Matthew from the moment Susie first mentioned him. I was a jealous and possessive child. The thought of Susie's divided affections was intolerable to me. Deep down I couldn't be sure that Susie didn't really prefer Matt, and that he wasn't nicer and more handsome. When she mentioned him I would lash out.

'Well – why don't you go and work for Matthew then,' I would say, 'if you like him so much?'

'Jack – you are not a nice boy when you say this thing. You don't know how lucky you are. You have a nice mother. You have a nice father. But you! You are too spoilt! You! You are not a nice boy. If you talk like this I go to your mom and I take my severance and I retire. I say I am finish with Jack.'

This was enough to do the trick; it was enough to make me sweet and contrite and lovable for the rest of the day and I would pick up my clothes and wash the dishes and make sweet tea whenever Susie asked.

Susie used to walk me to nursery school in the mornings and walk me home in the afternoons. Sometimes, when it rained, she called her friend Alfred to pick us up in his car so we wouldn't get soaked. She made my breakfast and prepared my school lunches. She made my bed every morning, tidied my room and washed my clothes. After every meal she washed the dishes, except the supper dishes that could wait until morning. She lived in a cottage at the back of the house. It was tidy, with a small garden and a stoep that overlooked the swimming pool. In the summer Susie would sit on the stoep and watch me swim while she sunned her legs.

'Come on, Susie! Come and swim!'

'I don't swim. I don't like it.'

'Come put your feet in the water.'

If it was hot enough, she could be tempted to remove her *tekkies* and dangle her feet in the shallow end of the pool while I did somersaults and handstands.

'You are a good swimmer,' Susie said as she laughed, 'but I don't like swimming.'

I splashed water at her.

'Jack – I am your mother. Don't do it.'

I am your mother: a curious phrase, but it made me happy. Both my parents had had occasion to say to me, 'Susie is not your slave,' and yet I loved Susie with the same possessive intensity that I loved my mother. Afterwards, after I betrayed her, I didn't like to hear that phrase any more. I didn't like it when she said, 'I am your mother.' Betraying someone is bad, of course, yet we all do it from time to time. But people don't betray their mothers.

I could not quite imagine how life would be possible without two mothers. There was so much that had to be done. Someone had to be home to greet me when I came back from school and someone had to listen and nod politely as I recounted the minutiae of my school day: 'Pietie was talking in class but Miss thought it was me and she told me to stand up and I said to her, "It wasn't me, Miss, it was Pietie." And then she said, "Don't be a tattletale. No one likes a tattletale." But I wasn't. And then she hit me on the hand with the ruler, Susie. Like this. Five times. And Pietie, I saw him, he laughed.' And then Susie would say, 'Mmm . . . that's nice, my baby.'

Someone had to make my bed and make me lunch. Someone had to tell the gardener what to do and make him lunch and someone had to iron the sheets. But mothers also needed to go out and work and have adventures and do exciting things in the world so that you didn't have to say that your mother was a housewife. It was embarrassing to say your mother was a housewife. Why, Thomas's mother was a radio personality and Emmanuel's mother was an accountant and Jürgen's mother had to run the family factory. My mother used to teach at the Hope School which was for handicapped children but she had a terrible row with the principal after my mother told a girl in a wheelchair that she was too dumb to go to university and the principal said my mother was 'prejudiced'. So now she taught English in an Afrikaans school instead.

But these were not the sorts of mothers that you wanted at home *all the time*. Nobody wanted an accountant overseeing how you spent your pocket money, or a teacher overseeing you do your homework. We needed mothers when we came home from school, but not mothers who took too keen an interest in what it was we did. We needed second-in-command mothers who could be told, 'It's OK, my mom said I'm allowed.' I liked having a mother who was warm and affectionate, who mollycoddled me, who gave me hugs all the time and told me how handsome I was and how clever I was and how sweet I was, but could also be asked to keep her distance. I don't like to think too much about what this excess of affection did to us as children – that is in addition to the unwarranted esteem of our *biological* parents. But there must have been precious few hours in our young lives where there wasn't a maternal presence of one kind or another.

I didn't have many chores, and those I did have, I got my sister Rachel to take on by bribing her with a game of Hi-Ho-Cherry-O. That Hi-Ho-Cherry-O happened to be the most enduring pleasure of my sister's childhood was propitious, for it also happened to be the singularly most monotonous game known to humankind. My sister loved it because it required no skill and the duplicity of older brothers would have no bearing on the outcome. A spinner in the centre of the board determined the number of cherries you could remove from your tree and deposit in a little plastic bucket. If you were the first to pick all your cherries, you were required to jump up, twirl like a ballerina and shout, 'Hi-Ho-Cherry-O!' You could not just say, 'I won,' for my sister's insistence on strict adherence to the rules would deny a win to the would-be victor if this final act of humiliation was not performed.

'You have to do it, Jack, otherwise you have to put all your cherries back on the tree and we start again.'

Root canal would be preferable to Hi-Ho-Cherry-O. The merest hint that someone, anyone, my mother, my father, Lisa, Susie, Nicola, anyone, might relent to a game of Hi-Ho-Cherry-O would cause much excitement and delight.

'Rachel, do you feel like a game of Hi-Ho-Cherry-O?' I would ask.

'Oh yes please!' she'd say.

'Take the washing off the line.'

'Can we play Hi-Ho-Cherry-O now, Jack?'

'Pick up the dog poops.'

'Can we play Hi-Ho-Cherry-O now, Jack?'

'Feed the cats.'

'Can we play Hi-Ho-Cherry-O now, Jack?'

'Never, Rachel. I will never, ever play that game with you. Ever.'

'But I took the washing off the line and I picked up the dog poops and I fed the cats.'

'So?'

'But you said! You promised!'

'I didn't say I *would* play Hi-Ho-Cherry-O, I just asked if you *felt* like playing.'

My sister quickly learnt that not only is the world cruel and unfair, but that things are worse, that when you are six and your most enduring pleasure is a game of Hi-Ho-Cherry-O the source of the cruelty and the unfairness is none other than your older brother, your hero, your protector.

This realisation revealed itself in the sharp intake of breath at the moment of betrayal, the stuttered words, 'but . . . but . . . but . . .', the insufferable sniffing, 'you . . . you . . . you . . .', immediately followed by my failed intervention 'Shut up, Rachel!' in the hope that I could avoid the piercing wail . . . 'But youuuuu saiiiiidddd' . . . that would summon Susie to the site of injustice.

'Jack – what you do to Rachel?' she asked.

'Nothing, Susie.'

'Rachel – what your brother do to you?'

'He . . . he . . . he made me pick up the dog poops and he . . . he . . . he made me take the washing off the line and he made me feed the cats and he promised to . . . to . . . to play Hi-Ho-Cherry-O . . .'

'Jack?'

'Yes, Susie?'

'This is not right. You are not fair. Your baby sister – she is so sweet. Why you do this thing? I see Rachel is picking up the dog poops – this *little girl* – and I think – why Rachel is doing this? I know your mommy say you must do this thing. Jack, this is not fair. You want me to tell your mother? I say to her, "Ruth, Jack, your son, is lazy. He is a lazy boy and he's not nice to his sister." Shame, Jack, she's a *little* girl.'

'Do you want to play with us, Susie?' I asked innocently.

'I am very busy.'

'Please, Susie, it will be fun,' I said with a smile.

My sister joined in. 'P – please . . . please, Su– Susie . . .'

'Jack, I hit you. Play with Rachel.'

Chastised, I said, 'All right – where's the board?'

'In my . . . my . . . bedroom. I put out all the cherries already, Jack. If you play with me you can be any colour – I promise, Jack. Except purple is my most favourite colour.'

She wiped her nose on her pinafore. 'What colour do you want to be, Jack?' she asked brightly.

'Purple.'

Sometimes, I would make two mugs of sweet tea and we would sit on her stoep while Susie told me about her child-hood in Kabalazani, a small village outside of Pretoria, where she and her cousin Michael were raised by their grandmother. Kabalazani was a *village*, Susie told me, not a township. It wasn't like Mamelodi or Soweto. These were townships and they were rough. And Kabalazani didn't have any shacks; there were no squatter camps in Kabalazani. Most of the houses had running water and many had electricity too. In Kabalazani people weren't interested in politics. They were interested in their gardens.

'One Christmas my granny she buys me a present. The next one she buys Michael a present. We were too poor, Jack. My mother she never give my granny money for me and my cousin. One Christmas my granny she buy me a dress. I love that dress, Jack. It was too beautiful. But Michael, that one, he was so jealous of me. You know what he does, Jack? I laugh. He take the dress and he cut it like this. He cut it up with the scissor. Yo yo yo! Jack, my heart was so sore when I see he do this thing. I was crying and crying and crying. That dress was so beautiful. I never have a dress like this one. I couldn't believe he would do this thing. And my granny, Jack – she was so mad. My granny – she is like your father – she has a big temper. She has a very big temper. She is so angry – she take Michael and she hit him.'

Susie could no longer contain her mirth and burst out laughing.

'She hit him, Jack, like this. Wha! Wha! Wha! On his

face, on his ear, and Michael he cries and he screams. I say, "Yes, Granny, you must hit this boy!" I say, "Hit him, Granny, hit him! He is a very bad boy!" And he cries, Jack! Michael he cries and he says, "No, Granny, it wasn't me! Granny it wasn't me, it was . . . it was –'" she gasped for breath, bent double from laughter – "'it was the tokoloshe, Granny!'"

Tears ran down her cheeks, which she wiped away with the back of her hand.

'Jack, I never saw my granny hit anyone like she hit Michael. She was so mad with this one. One day you must meet Michael and you must ask him about this thing. Yo yo yo, Jack, he will laugh if you ask him about this thing. He will remember. You must ask him about this thing. Michael – he was a very naughty boy. But he makes me laugh.'

I was not exactly sure what it was that Susie found so funny about this; the fact that she didn't really believe in the tokoloshe or that Michael would be so foolish as to invoke the wrath of the tokoloshe for something the creature was not responsible for. When I first asked about the tokoloshe – I couldn't have been older than five or six – Susie said, 'It's . . . a monster. He's a small monster – an evil spirit.'

'Like a ghost?'

'No, not like a ghost. Like a monster. In the village, the old people put their bed on bricks so the tokoloshe can't get them when they sleep.'

'Is it for real?' I asked.

'What you mean?'

'The tokoloshe – is he for real?'

'The people say so.'

'Does he attack people?'

'Yes, he eat your face.'

'Really?' I said.

'Yes.'

'Does he eat *white* people's faces?'

'Ha ha – you scared of the tokoloshe, my baby?'

'No . . . but is he for real, *for real*, Susie?'

'That's what the people say.'

'Can't people catch him?'

'He's magic.'

'But you can shoot him with a gun. My friend's father has a gun. If he saw the tokoloshe he would shoot him. You can even kill an elephant with a gun but not a .22.'

'He's too powerful that one. Too too powerful.'

'Do you really believe in the tokoloshe, Susie?'

'That's what people say.'

'Don't tease me. Should we put some bricks under my bed?'

'Jack,' she snapped, 'if you make mess in your bedroom I will hit you!'

Everything Susie said seemed foreign to me and must have laid the foundation of my prejudiced belief that all black people are afflicted by the certain tragedy of their fates. How terrible to be separated from your mother, to live with a tyrannical grandmother in a house with cow-dung floors. I thought, too, what I might have done, were I there when Michael ruined Susie's Christmas; the mean-spiritedness of the whole thing enraged me. Blessed with foreknowledge, I would have followed Michael into the room and caught him red-handed. I would have said, 'Michael, what are you doing with Susie's dress?' and punched him for good measure. Michael would have been scared of me and done anything I told him to, because I was white and Michael was black. And sometimes, though it might have been terrible in ways I did not grasp, being powerful for no reason was a good thing.

It also occurred to me, much later, after I had heard this story many times, that there were other ways to right this injustice, to intervene before the calamitous event that would spoil Christmas for a poor little black girl living in a shack house with dung floors. I could take my money and buy Michael a present, perhaps a toy car or a gun. Not only could I buy him a present, but also, believing myself a sensitive and considerate child, I could give the present to his grandmother so that Michael would never know that I had interceded on his behalf and saved him from his most disgraceful impulses. And Susie's grandmother would say, 'Thank you, Jack, you are a good boy. You are so nice to the black people. You love the black people too much. Thank you, Jack. God loves you.' And while I thought about these things, Susie fished in her overalls for her snuffbox. Snuff was her only guilty habit that I knew of, though as unpleasant habits go, it was pretty revolting. 'Snuff is too bad,' she would say, 'but I have a big headache.'

2

Jesus and the KGB

ON THE JOURNEYS to and from school, the navy safari suit that all the boys in my primary school had to wear chafed uncomfortably against my thighs. The knee-high socks with the gold-and-blue bands slid down to my ankles and every few blocks I would stop to tug them up to my knees. The safari suit was something of an anachronism, for most schools had long since abandoned it for grey pants with short- or long-sleeved shirts, depending on the season. However, the principal, an Englishman in the sense that he actually came from England, believed that the colonies could not comprehend the meaning of the word 'tradition' and as such would never appreciate the full gravity of change, in the British sense of the word, unless they were subjected to its absurdities for a few decades. The streets in my suburb were lined with jacaranda trees. In the spring and early summer, the pavement was always covered in purple fluted flowers that made it slippery underfoot. The trees were infested with spitting beetles, which nestled in the upper branches and secreted odorous saliva that dripped onto the pavement below. Pushing a friend into the slow dribble of spit was a favourite activity.

My eleventh birthday marked a significant milestone in my schooling. I had spent an equal amount of time in Afrikaans and English schools, so it followed that this was the one point in my life when, unlike my parents, I was equally English and Afrikaans. No length of time would change the fact that my father was a Boer and my mother a *rooinek*. I was at the time in an English primary school. Unless something dramatic happened I was set upon an inexorable path to Englishness. Englishness, of course, in the South African sense, which my principal Mr Harrison would have pointed out, was very far removed from Englishness proper. But this was not always so. I had thought I would grow up Afrikaans. The reason for this unexpected turn was a small misunderstanding of the intractable sort.

The principal of my former Afrikaans school, a staunch and humourless Nationalist, was obsessed (even beyond what might normally be expected of the time) with the unique threat that communism posed to South Africa and her sub-Saharan neighbours. An American evangelical pastor had given him a book about the ordeal of a Christian soldier in the Soviet Union who had defected to the United States. Mr Bloom was so moved by this tale of torture and Soviet wickedness that he spent several months translating key passages into Afrikaans, so that he might share these revelations with the community at large. He was a regular speaker at the Women's Federation, Bible Groups of all denominations (bar Catholics) and the Voortrekkers. (If you were English you went to Cubs or Scouts or Brownies or Guides. If you were Afrikaans you went to the Voortrekkers. I did know one Afrikaans child who joined the Scouts. When his grandfather found out he marched into the Scout hall and dragged Brandt out by his ears. Did he not know that the Scouting movement was founded during the Boer War? Old enmities aside, his grandfather did him a favour. Everyone knew Scouts was for faggots.)

There were rumours that a local publishing house was interested in Mr Bloom's translation and were in negotiations with the reformed communist who had, perhaps a little too quickly for their liking, adopted all things American, including a hard-nosed attitude to business. But Mr Bloom's first and most loyal audience was his pupils. His weekly instalments had become the highlight of our morning assemblies.

"'The Russians,'" Mr Bloom read, "'will do anything to break the spirit of the Christian. Many people have asked why I simply did not denounce God and the Christian faith to my torturers while maintaining my inner beliefs. Surely, they argue, this would have been the sensible thing to do. God would have forgiven you, they say. But would I have forgiven myself? And, if I had betrayed my saviour, would I have had the strength to endure weeks in the Soviet winter with nothing to sustain me? I would have given up my only source of warmth: my burning love for Jesus Christ. So enraged were they, so lonely and confused, that they vented their wrath upon my weak body. They broke my legs. They broke my arms. They fractured my skull. And when they were done, my eyes were swollen shut. They had no choice but to carry me back to the barracks; an act of tenderness brought about by their own savagery. Cradled in the arms of these powerful soldiers, my love for these men grew.'"

The Soviets were of particular interest to me and my friends who, having formed a gang called 'The Gang', needed to devise a set of tasks for potential recruits to ascertain whether they were possessed of sufficient courage and stamina. The KGB was the gold standard, the measure of cunning and ruthlessness, to which we aspired. And so it was that in whispers, excited giggles and the general din of the playground snatches of conversations reached the ears of Miss Swanepoel, our teacher, who mistook it all for an unwarranted fear which might spoil the innocent abandon of childhood.

'The principal is entirely correct,' she said one morning, having decided to put our minds at ease, 'in telling you about the dangers of the communists. Communism is the work of the devil. However, there is nothing to worry about. If Russia ever went to war with South Africa, we would most certainly win. South Africa has God on its side.'

She said this as if God's allegiance was a fact, like one of the exports listed in the geography textbook, and our rapt attention pleased her. She must have thought it exhilarating to have added a theological addendum to our headmaster's instalments. What Miss Swanepoel said was not in any way controversial, but I am certain Mr Bloom would have considered it presumptuous. Having just graduated from teachers training college, she was a *junior* and not expert in matters of politics or religion. So she looked a little flushed when she said this, as if she had been a touch too daring for her own good. And indeed, she had, for Miss Swanepoel had just carelessly sundered certain and insuperable barriers. The insubstantial world of Father Christmas and the KGB and crucifixions and everything else that existed, but not really, not then and certainly not there, came crashing rudely into the world of school and parents and The Gang. There was no telling how far the invasion had advanced, or what lengths the KGB would go to in accomplishing their dastardly ambitions. There was not time to consider in a scientific way the military efficacy of plagues versus the atomic bomb. The uncomfortable feeling in my stomach, a thrashing hollowness, grew until it was too big to be contained and pushed its way through what I now know to be the cardiac sphincter, creating a slight pressure on my sternum before working its way up the oesophagus to my mouth, where like a belch it erupted in an ill-considered statement of allegiance that pealed across the classroom: 'I'm with the Russians.'

This was how I first learnt that a childish outburst can avalanche beyond one's imaginings, because a week later an extra three blocks had been added to my school journey, my maroon-and-gold-banded socks were exchanged for blue-and-gold ones, and my future self had been changed irrevocably. I was certain to grow up English. If my parents took any pride in this incident, thinking perhaps that their son had suddenly shown himself possessed of a certain courage or moral fibre, they could not have been more mistaken. The incident revealed two things about my character: cowardice and a tendency to do what was expedient. The latter was a very South African characteristic and the reason why, despite being raised by atheists, I prayed in times of mortal danger or when only the intercession of the Almighty could alter circumstances in my favour.

I had no objections to growing up English. I knew that my father's reluctance (not complete unwillingness) to resort to corporal punishment, the family's tendency to eat too many meals in restaurants and our absolute conviction that man was descended from apes, militated against us ever being Afrikaners in the true sense of the word. What was undeniable, though, was that the Afrikaans side of my family could wipe the floor with my English relatives.

You only had to look at my uncle, the physics professor, to know this. He had, in the twenty years of his tenure, achieved a notoriety that only a certain kind of professor would be proud of. Because physics was a compulsory subject for medicine, engineering, dentistry and veterinary science, he was the gatekeeper of the professional classes. Until you had passed Physics 101, that comfortable practice in the northern suburbs of Johannesburg was nothing but a mirage in the hostile terrain of my uncle's thousand-seat lecture hall. I had a mortal fear of the man and so, I suspect, did my father. So though it was fair to say that I had no objections to growing up English, I was aware that this would come at a cost; that the South African English were softer and weaker and I would never be able to inspire in others the terrible awe and fear that my uncle, with the merest glance and without uttering a word, was capable of.

My grandmother was undoubtedly the main source of my Afrikaans-ness. I remember being surprised the first time I saw her without a wig. She had short, thin, wispy hair like a baby. Her skin was soft and translucent and shot through with dark blue veins.

Old-age homes were not like hospitals. Old-age homes were neither tragic nor serious. They were simply boring. Visitors to old-age homes were always impatient to escape. Fingers drummed and feet tapped. People got up and adjusted curtains and sat down again. They got up to adjust television sets and sat down again. They moved vases and sat down again.

Ouma shared a room with another woman who

couldn't talk and smelt of urine. The other woman never had any visitors and often moaned and cried. It was very embarrassing and I wished they would move her because everyone had to pretend they couldn't hear, even when she was moaning very loudly. Everything about dying was embarrassing. For instance, when Ouma said, 'I will be with Jesus soon,' it was embarrassing because nobody knew what to say. We didn't know what to say because it was true and as much as one could tease a person to show that one loved them, it would be rude and it would hurt their feelings if one said, 'Yes, it is true. Soon you will be dead.' But it was a fact. My grandmother would soon be dead and it was right to be embarrassed when she said these things because there was nothing one could do about it.

My mother was not fond of Ouma. Though we visited her regularly, Ouma always greeted my mother first and said, 'How wonderful to see you. It's such a surprise.' And afterwards my mother would say, 'She is a very irritating woman.'

The reasons for Ouma's dislike were multifarious, but the fact that my mother was English and that she spoke Afrikaans badly, with a pronounced accent, did not play a small part. It was a family joke that my mother owed her pass in first-year Afrikaans literature to an exceptionally short skirt and a winning smile. All my mother remembered from Afrikaans lectures were four lines from a famous poem: *Raka, die aap-mens, hy wat nie kan dink, | wat swart and donker is, van been en spier | 'n lenige boog, en enkeld dier. (Raka, the ape-man, incapable of thought, | Dark and unknown, of muscle and bone | A solitary beast, a bow strung taut.)*

Ouma had false teeth that were too big for her mouth.

'Why don't we buy Ouma new false teeth?' I asked.

'I don't think Ouma wants new false teeth,' my mother said.

'They move when she talks.'

'I think Ouma is too old to go to the dentist.'

It seemed that one of the advantages of false teeth was that it obviated the need to go to a dentist at all. Surely one could simply remove the teeth and ask for a smaller size? This was appealing to a child like me who suffered from dental phobia. I thought about Ouma's teeth a great deal, but I didn't discuss the matter further. I knew, even then, that there was something unseemly in arguing about false teeth. As for the wig, it had been a source of endless amusement since Ouma first put it on backwards. Now it was kept on a polystyrene head in the small cupboard in her room at the old-age home. One could, I thought, carve a hole into the polystyrene head as a place to keep her dentures.

Ouma was my last tenuous connection to my Afrikaans family. When she was well enough to live on her own, her birthday was the one day of the year when the Afrikaans side of my family had a reunion of sorts. These were plenteous affairs in which the Afrikaner's overcompensation for a lean history was always in evidence: roast pork, roast beef, roast lamb, yellow rice with raisins, roast potatoes, chicken pie, game pie, green salad, potato salad with egg and peas, pumpkin fritters, dried sausage, biltong, mealie meal, onion and tomato sauce, jelly, ice cream, milk tarts and cake all washed down with Coke or Fanta for the children and beer or coffee for the adults. And afterwards my stomach would hurt, and it would be hard to breathe, so I would lie in the sun on the patch of grass in front of my cousin's house, thinking that maybe when the pain went away I could have another slice of banana loaf. My cousin's father, the mad psychiatrist with his big mad eyes, would tap his bloated stomach and look at his guests who were now both drunk and nauseous. And my uncle the physicist would look upon my uncle the psychiatrist with contempt and say to himself (or so I believed), 'Another year before I have to lay eyes on that dreadful man again. Another year before I have to tolerate my dreadful sister.'

When my uncle the physicist smiled, I admired his big shiny white teeth, every single one of which was titanium, carefully implanted by a former student. In addition to my uncle the physicist and my uncle the psychiatrist, my uncle the paedophile was also in attendance. I was allowed to talk to him because he had a predilection for girls rather than boys. Interestingly, this fact seemed to mitigate people's aversion for the man. I disliked him intensely. At the last party he had chased my cousin and me around the garden after we poked a pin in his bottom.

My aunts sat by their husbands, solicitously tending to them as they baked in the sun. And at the centre of it all sat Ouma, with a blanket over her legs, the dying matriarch who held in uneasy orbit this clan of angry, ambitious Afrikaners, each tearing into their meat with shiny sharp teeth.

When I was still in Afrikaans school I would visit my cousin Lourens on weekends. My mad psychiatrist uncle, enormous stomach and thin legs, would join us in the swimming pool. He chased us around and dunked us in the deep end until I, genuinely terrified, gasped for air. Everything the mad psychiatrist thought fun for young boys, I found frightening, including Saturday outings to the mine dumps south of the city. My mother did not like these trips. Abandoned mineshafts lay in wait for

35

foolish children who didn't watch where they put their feet.

'*Kom, kom!*' my cousin shouted as he raced to the top of the soft yellow dune at least six or seven storeys high. We thought it a mountain. It was hot and it burnt our feet. Steel carcasses of rusted mining equipment were silhouetted against the pale blue sky. I fell down and got a mouthful of sand, cyanide sand, and spat it out, brushing my tongue with my hand.

'It's poison. There's poison in the sand!'

My cousin laughed. 'I guess you're going to die then!'

Hysterically whooping, we ran around the top of the mine dump, picking up handfuls of sand and throwing it into the air.

It took the death of four friends to put an end to these trips for good. They had burrowed into the side of the dump and while sitting inside to admire their cave it collapsed. As one of the parents dug to free them, more sand slipped down the dune and they suffocated in the hot mine dumps of Johannesburg. Sand filled their eyes and their nostrils and their mouths. Could they feel the man's hands? Did they know he was trying to dig them out? Why did he give up? Did he just sit there on the mine dump and cry? Did he leave their bodies burning in the hot sand while he ran to look for help?

Their story had been told to the South African public in *You Magazine*, also published in Afrikaans as *Die Huisgenoot*. It was the closest thing we had to a tabloid so my parents did not buy it, but occasionally my best friend Petrus would lend me a copy so that I could pore over the lurid details of a tragedy that had befallen a family who covered their furniture in plastic and hung Van Gogh posters in the living room. Petrus loved *You Magazine* and bought it religiously every week. Our favourite story came in two parts and was about four brothers who were carrying a catamaran to the beach. The mast hit some power lines and all four boys lost an arm; two of the boys their left and the other two boys their right. The first part detailed the tragedy itself and included a picture taken moments before disaster struck. The editors had drawn a red circle around the top of the mast and a red circle around the power lines. In a moment they would be lying unconscious with black and blistered arms. That photo must have tormented them. Surely they wanted to shout out to their former selves, 'Watch out! The mast! You're going to hit the power lines!' The next part showed how all the boys had been fitted with prosthetic arms that had interchangeable hands and hooks. There was a photo of the boys sitting around the dinner table, smiling and laughing, learning to eat with their prostheses. The raw mechanics of the prostheses contrasted sharply with their handsome Afrikaner faces and soft sun-bleached hair. It was a compelling photograph and beautiful. 'What a pity,' Petrus said, 'their hooks are so ugly.'

I fantasised about befriending these four celebrities and thought about them whenever I walked past our local prosthetist's. It was unpleasant to see those pink limbs, those obscene simulacra, and to be reminded of car crashes and diabetes and war. Everyone was relieved when the shopkeeper died of a brain tumour and his wife closed the business.

I had no sense of how many people practised this peculiar profession. I thought it sufficiently rare to make an encounter with these boys, if not probable, then at least possible. As repellent as I found them, I would never look strangely at their hooks. It was poetic that they all suffered the same fate at the same time. The intimacy that exists between brothers could only be deepened. If they all walked in a line there would be a perfect symmetry of brothers and prostheses and, so as not to upset the balance, I would walk in the middle, two brothers on either side. People would say, 'Jack is their best friend. Those boys love Jack as if he were their own brother.'

When a terrible tragedy befell a boy my age, scarring him, crippling him, I thought him ennobled and beautiful, but this was not so with old people. There could be no tragedy, no overcoming. It didn't pain people's hearts to see an old woman in a wheelchair. It might be sad, but there was no poetry. They were just old and no longer beautiful. This, you see, was why people put so much money into that polio girl's head. They stuffed great wads of cash into that slit, because she was only eight or nine or thereabouts, and had a nasty-looking leg brace and she clutched a sad blue teddy bear. Everyone was very moved by the polio girl even though she and her teddy were made of fibreglass.

When Ouma fell pregnant she married my grandfather, a schoolteacher, and they had eight children. They lived in a small town called Smithfield in the south of the Orange Free State, the most conservative and backward of the provinces. Three of the children died. That was the way it seemed to be with Afrikaners. Like frogs and millipedes and things, they had lots of children because so many of them died. The only one of the dead siblings I knew anything about was Dead Daphne, who gave her pocket money to the blind. I once heard my aunt refer to her as 'Fucking Dead Daphne' which everyone thought was very funny, but they would never have said this to Ouma's face because Dead Daphne was her favourite child. My mother attributed this to the fact that Dead Daphne was only twelve when she died and so she didn't have time to grow up and do unpleasant things and irritate Ouma like the rest of her children had. Dead Daphne was the reason that Ouma made an exception for Jewish doctors. It was an Afrikaans doctor who failed to diagnose tetanus and from that day forward she maintained that all Afrikaans doctors were quacks.

But the dead children were not the end of the family's misery. My grandfather went mad and chased his family out of the house with an axe. They returned three days later to find his body in the garage. He had gassed himself. About the matter my father said, 'It was terribly embarrassing.' They moved to Krugersdorp just outside of Johannesburg and Ouma worked as a matron at the boarding school where they also lived. I wanted to ask my father what was most embarrassing: the fact that his father killed himself, the fact that they lived in a boarding school or the fact that his mother was a matron? All of these things would be embarrassing, but surely worst of all would be attending the school where your mother was the matron.

Ouma was a staunch Nationalist and absolutely mad for Pik Botha, the Minister of Foreign Affairs. Sometimes I got confused between Pik Botha and P.W. Botha who was the president. My father said that at least Ouma liked the better of the two Bothas. Pik wasn't good, but the president was evil. P.W. Botha used to wear a bowler hat and wagged his finger when he was angry. He also used to lick his lips. Pik Botha never wore hats and never licked his lips. Also, he had a thick black moustache and shiny black hair. My grandmother thought Pik was very *debonair*

– 'My,' she said, 'but he's very *debonair*.' My mother said he looked like a second-hand car salesman. He became famous for saying that South Africa was like a zebra and that it didn't matter if you shot it through the black stripe or the white stripe, it would still be dead. Pik also once made P.W. very angry by saying he would agree to serve under a black president. This happened while Pik was overseas. It was a little bit like saying 'fuck' in front of your friends – for a while it seemed like a very brave, very manly thing to do, but unless you were prepared to say it in front of your mother it didn't mean much at all. And when Pik was back in front of P.W., well, he changed his story pretty quickly. But Ouma really loved him. In fact, she loved him so much she wrote him a letter telling him what a marvellous politician he was and Pik replied with a bouquet of flowers, which, when you think about it, was a pretty nice thing to do. Since that day nothing could dim her passion for the man. Ouma had had the required quota of grief to make most quirks permissible; mild anti-Semitism, mild racism – nothing rampant or unseemly, nothing undignified. Age had mellowed her, weathered away opinions and, quiet and accepting, resigned to death, her focus narrowed to Jesus. Watching her on the bed in the old-age home, my memory darted back to a time when my grandmother was still living on her own. She looked graceful that day, wearing a brown suit and lemon blouse. She was perched on the end of the settee, holding her teacup and staring out of the window.

'I see your family is here,' said Matron as she walked into the room. 'It's very good to see you again.' She gestured towards the woman who moaned all the time and asked, 'Is Mrs Read bothering you? Don't mind Mrs Read – Mrs Read is deaf as a doornail. Poor thing is nearly blind too – but what can you do? Your mother is looking well, isn't she? Mrs Viljee is our favourite resident in the home. We hardly hear a peep out of her. Isn't that right, Mrs Viljee?'

3

Killing the first-borns

IN ADDITION TO being my best friend, Petrus was my walking companion on the journey to and from school. I had known Petrus at my old school but never befriended him because Petrus was a *moffie* on account of the fact that he played with girls and acted like them too. But now that we weren't in the same school, it was safe to spend the afternoons at each other's houses. My new English school was only a little further than the Afrikaans school and Petrus lived a few minutes' walk from my house. He was tall and thin with wavy blond hair and light blue eyes. He had a gentle, effeminate manner. His sister was an air hostess for South African Airways and through her he developed a flawed but endearing discernment about all the things in the world to which he had, and only ever would have, the most tangential connection. He might say, 'South African Airways is the second-best airline in the world. It's better than British Airways, but not as good as Swissair. Everyone knows that Swissair is the best,' or, 'If you are very rich, you go to Switzerland on holiday.

Switzerland has the best skiing in the world. But if you are not so rich, then you can go to Mauritius. Mauritius is the poor man's Mediterranean.'

Petrus's family was *so* Afrikaans his mother kept chickens in the backyard. She used benzene to burn the hairs off slaughtered birds, which, mixed with the aroma of a stew large enough to feed ten or fifteen people, created a thick oily stench that hung in the house. It always seemed as if Afrikaners were preparing for the worst. It was unthinkable for Petrus's family to buy a regular bottle of tomato sauce or a small bag of sugar when MAKRO could supply you with ten-litre vats or fifteen-kilogram bags. They would make their way home in their Datsun half-ton bakkie, laden with food (Petrus seated in the back holding on to the boxes like a farmhand), as if war was imminent or indeed another trek, this time further north, away from the rising tide of angry blacks. Maputo could become Lourenço Marques once again if the whites drove out the black communists. This was not impossible. The president of Mozambique, Samora Machel, died because the Russians who were flying the plane were drunk, even though everyone blamed South Africa and said we crashed his plane on purpose. They said we *assassinated* him, like JFK. But it wasn't like Portugal could become cross with South Africa for interfering with Mozambique because they said they didn't want it any more, and anyway, there were lots of Portuguese people living in South Africa. You only had to walk into a greengrocer or a corner shop to see that there was almost a village of Porras who lived above it or beside it.

What I liked most about Petrus was his willingness to tell me everything about his family. I had developed a voyeur's interest in the goings-on of the Steyn household, including his parents Oom Frik and Tannie Vera (we referred to most people over the age of eighteen as *oom* – uncle – or *tannie* – auntie). I knew, for instance, that Petrus's mother, Tannie Vera, had walked in on his sister having sex with her boyfriend and that his brother, Anton, shot the neighbour's dog with a 9mm Magnum. And though Petrus never said as much, I understood Petrus was the cause of some tension in the household. I had seen for myself how his father, Oom Frik, sat glumly in the corner as his son paraded around wearing the orange-and-blue sash of the National Party. Oom Frik had been a loyal member of the regional committee since 1972 and although he was rendered mute by the provenance of the offending garment, the election was only a brief respite, for as Petrus grew older his new adult body and deep bari-tone voice brought his peculiarities into sharp relief. But in standard four, a few months before his twelfth birthday, I imagine his parents told themselves, and almost believed, that Petrus was merely sensitive, that his affectations did not signal a carnality they thought monstrous.

Though Petrus and I spent a great deal of time at each other's houses, our best times together were spent walking to and from school, which in the afternoons could take hours even though the journey was less than two miles. He waited for me at the top of my block in the mornings and then outside his school gates in the afternoons, so that we might continue our discussions about all the things that interested us. At the time we were fascinated by the arrival of our suburb's only non-European resident. The woman was Chinese and had never been seen without her black umbrella. Behind a fence that I thought perilously low, she kept two aggressive Dobermanns. Whenever we crossed the boundary that demarcated the stretch of pavement in front of the Chinese woman's house, the dogs exploded in a frenzy of growling and barking. I would whistle tunelessly lest the animals think me in any way perturbed. The Chinese woman would emerge, umbrella in hand, and shout what we believed to be Chinese obscenities at her dogs. Then she would turn back into the house, muttering furiously, and slam the door behind her.

Our first line of questioning concerned the reason why she had left China in the first place. Petrus said, 'Maybe it's because she doesn't want to eat her dogs. In China they eat dogs like they were chickens. I know because my sister told me. Do you think she's Taiwanese or Chinese?'

'How does one tell the difference?' I asked.

'The Chinese are communists,' Petrus replied authoritatively.

I thought dog-eating possible though not probable, even if it might explain why the Chinese woman was living in our neighbourhood. My mother told me that the Chinese used to be treated like blacks until there was a slump in sugar exports. The Chinese bought a lot of sugar, and in recognition of their contribution to the South African economy, the government negotiated a deal with the communists in which all Chinese people would, from that day forward, be 'honorary whites' and in return shiploads of sugar would continue to make their way across the Indian Ocean. It was no surprise that they bought a lot of sugar. In Chinese restaurants they had a dessert called 'bowties' which was the sweetest and most delicious thing I had ever eaten. The woman peered from behind her curtains and I tried to smile at her. I appreciated that she made the effort to shout at her dogs. Even though she was Chinese she understood it was rude when your dogs barked at people. Particularly white people.

Although Petrus and I agreed about a great many things, there were tensions and disagreements between us also. Petrus loved the National Party because his mother took him to tea parties and fund-raisers and meetings and other glamorous adult things and he would always return home with handfuls of rosettes and sashes and the like. And so Petrus would ask if I wanted to help him and his father put up posters for the National Party, to which I would respond, 'The National Party is bad.' And then Petrus, mildly indignant, would say, 'Says who?'

'Everyone knows they're bad.' I could not simply say, 'My parents.'

'It's fun putting up posters. My father will buy you a Coke and some chips. He says if I help put up one hundred posters he will give me five rand.'

This of course would pique my interest, so I would say, 'Can we put up posters for the DP instead?' And Petrus would consider this carefully for a while before asking, 'Which ones are they?'

'The blue ones with a little bit of yellow.'

'I'll ask my father.'

If five rand was at stake it probably wouldn't have mattered who we were putting up posters for. For five rand my eleven-year-old self would have joined the Hitler Youth.

Other than the National and Democratic Parties, there was the Conservative Party, which was mainly yellow with some blue. It was sad but true that my physicist uncle voted for the Conservative Party. This fact pained my father and it pained me too. I admired my uncle very much. The problem with supporting the Conservative Party, I decided, was that it erased everything good about my uncle. It erased the fact that he was a good scientist and a good teacher. It erased the fact that he gave up afternoons and weekends

47

to teach dumb kids who struggled with maths or science. There are certain things that a lifetime of good deeds could not make up for, and supporting the Conservative Party was one of them.

There were many reasons why the Conservative Party was bad, but the thing I thought most terrible about them was that they loved putting people to death. When we drove past Pretoria Central Prison, I would sit up and press my nose against the window of our VW Kombi and think about the facts I knew about executions: Pretoria Central Prison hanged people on Monday mornings at 7 a.m.; up to seven people could be hanged at one time; there were fifty-two steps which led to the death chamber; the night before the execution, prisoners were given a roast chicken to eat; when the judge sentenced the prisoner he said, 'You are sentenced to be taken hence to the prison, something, something, and then to a place of execution, to be hanged by the neck until you are dead, something, something, and may the Lord have mercy upon your soul.' The sentence actually reads: 'You are sentenced to be taken hence to the prison in which you were last confined and from there to a place of execution where you will be hanged by the neck until dead and thereafter your body buried within the precincts of the prison and may the Lord have mercy upon your soul.' The words were terrible and beautiful. For instance, I liked the way they said 'a place of execution' when they knew very well that they were taking you to Pretoria. But it wouldn't sound nearly as poetic to say, 'We're going to take you to Pretoria and hang you.' I was fascinated by these words but was incapable of committing them to memory. I wanted to ask my father to write them down but I knew he would think this strange. I did not want him to say, 'Don't be so obsessive, Jack.' Perhaps the fascination lay not only in the poetry, but also the magic, the power they conveyed, as if their utterance were intractable and their effect inexorable. It was as if the second part of the sentence regretted the first, making a half-hearted attempt to call back the very thing it had set into motion. Of course this was not true. There was one man who could undo it all. P.W. Botha (the one with the bowler hat, who licked his lips) could stop an execution at any time. He could *commute* your sentence. So even if one did not like P.W. Botha, even though he had a bulbous head and fat, fleshy lips, even though he was cruel, one could not but respect someone who had power over life and death.

When my father was still a young advocate, before he worked for banks and mines and insurance companies, he defended a man who was sentenced to death. Joseph Mabena chopped up two women with a machete and hid the body parts in the veld outside of Johannesburg. My father visited him the day before the sentence was carried out, but declined to witness the execution. This was right. It would have been very wrong to watch a man die. Besides, my father didn't even like to use ant spray.

Sometimes I lay awake at night thinking what it would be like to be executed. It was conceivable that I might face the death sentence one day. I could be wrongly accused or, in a moment of madness, kill someone. And I thought about these things before, long before, I knew how easy it was to do bad things, in a careless and unthinking way. I had a strong sense that the universe was setting up nasty traps for me, all sorts of really horrible ways to die in which I would in some way be complicit in my own demise. Perhaps if I was in any way astute, it was in respect of my own character. They left you in a room to kill you.

You could shout and cry as much as you liked, it made no difference at all. It was the one time you could be sure that no one would ever help you. My mother could stand behind the glass crying but even she wouldn't be able to help. Living in a world in which my execution, though improbable, still remained possible, upset me. I very much wanted them to abolish the death penalty. And for this reason, I could not forgive my uncle. My uncle voted for the Conservative Party and they loved putting people to death. If it came to it, they would even kill me.

Petrus would have made a better brother to Rachel than I could ever have managed. She adored him and I suspect he adored her too. If Petrus and I were playing in the pool and she asked if she could join, Petrus would always protest if I sent her away. If Petrus went to the kitchen to make sandwiches, he'd find Rachel and ask if she wanted sandwiches too. If no one wanted to play Hi-Ho-Cherry-O with Rachel, she would wait patiently for Petrus to visit because he'd always say yes and would never dare ask to be purple (even though it was his favourite colour too). I found the two of them one day climbing the willow tree which grew behind the garage. Because Rachel was a bit squat she wasn't a good tree climber, but seeing Petrus and me high in the tree would send her into a state of desperate excitement. And so Petrus taught her all the tricks we'd discovered through painful falls and scraped knees. 'Be careful, Rachie, put your foot in that hole over there and hold with your hand over here. Don't worry, I'm right behind you. I'll catch you if you fall.'

He'd throw loose change in the pool and they would have competitions to see who could dive out the most. He won at this game just enough not to make her suspicious and not so often as to make her disheartened. Beating Petrus at this game was an achievement, but not impossible. When my sister named the Kreepy-Krauly pool cleaner 'Pickles' he played along and said, 'OK, if we're going to have a race we need to move Pickles first.' Sometimes their closeness made me a little jealous but I told myself it was because he didn't have to see her all the time. If Petrus had to live with Rachel, as I did, he would quickly tire of her. But I think it also had something to do with the fact that he was the youngest in his family and that Rachel was a girl.

Petrus arranged a trip for the three of us to go to the Boswell Wilkie Circus. Rachel had been looking forward to it for weeks because she'd never been to a circus before. I had no desire to go. My mother thought circuses were common and I thought she was right. My father thought circuses were cruel and I thought he was right too. But Rachel was so excited and Petrus had gone to so much trouble to arrange this trip that they bit their tongues. And so did I. Petrus's brother picked us up in his yellow Land Rover and dropped us off outside the tent on a Saturday afternoon. I noticed with dismay that the place was swarming with children from Brixton and Mayfair. Most of them were too poor to pay for tickets so they hung around the elephant enclosure and tried to sneak into the tent when the circus workers weren't looking. If one of the workers caught a child, he'd drag him out by his collar while the kid screamed, 'Fuck you – you *mund*! Get your fucking *mund* hands off me!' and the worker would cuff the child around the back of the head and the kid would scream, 'Wait till I tell my brother. He'll come round with a gun and fuck you up, *lekker*!'

Petrus said it was funny that Mayfair was rough because in London Mayfair was fancy. And there was a Brixton in London too but he didn't know much about it. I couldn't imagine a place called Mayfair being fancy. It was almost as bad as Brixton – though everyone knew Brixton was worse because that's where they put the Brixton Murder and Robbery Squad. Of course it wasn't only for murders and robberies in Brixton but people said, 'It's pretty conveniently located.' Lots of stories in *You Magazine* were about people who lived in Brixton and Mayfair. There was even a story about a woman in Mayfair who breast-fed her poodle and when I told my mother she didn't believe me. 'I promise,' I said. 'I saw it in *You Magazine*,' but she just said, 'Nonsense. And where did you get a *You Magazine*?'

I noticed Chad, one of the boys from my school, standing by the elephant enclosure. Chad was thirteen and in standard five. Everybody knew he lived in Mayfair Boys' Home, the orphanage. He was wearing a tattered pair of shorts and a singlet. He had smooth brown limbs and was handsome. Tucked behind his ear was a cigarette. I was embarrassed to be with Petrus and my sister. Chad was hard and beautiful. I was soft and spoilt. I was wearing a new pair of Wranglers and a shirt from Edgars that cost a lot of money. My mother had stuffed wads of cash in my pocket. I was sure Chad's parents were dead because it was impossible that anyone could have given up a child this beautiful. His name was as appealing as his good looks. How magnificent that his parents, before they died, should give him *that* name – an American name, a name for movie stars and rock musicians. Amazing that these things could just be done. Chad. In a world full of Petruses and Johanneses and Brandts and Steyns and Erensts and Emils how very refreshing, how very exotic. Chad was sporty too.

He played soccer and cricket for the A team. People said his schoolwork was as tidy as the tidiest, the most studious of girls – but this never placed him under suspicion of *moffie-ness,* for his prowess on the sporting field served to dispel any such aspersions. At the age of eleven I didn't have any specific ideas about what I would like to do with Chad – proximity to this fine individual would be sufficient. It was only when I was much older that I realised proximity was a very poor substitute for a good fuck.

Chad was in charge of all the children from Mayfair Boys' Home. He wasn't a prefect because the teachers knew he smoked, even though he didn't do it at school. Besides, it was rare for a boy from the orphanage to be a prefect. But if they'd wanted to choose a child whose discipline would be absolute, they couldn't have chosen better than Chad. I wanted to leave Petrus and my sister and go and play with these kids in the dirt, but they probably wouldn't have had me anyway.

We watched the circus, which was as horrible as I thought it would be. The elephants seemed tranquillised. The lions looked tatty. Women did tricks on horseback, but they were too old to be wearing shiny bikinis and I could see one had false teeth, because they moved a bit when she came down hard on the horse. They sweated beneath their make-up, trying so hard to please the few people in the audience. The 'World Famous Russian Acrobats' dropped one another, twice, but it wasn't exciting because there were safety nets. Everyone knew real acrobats didn't have safety nets. And it turned out they weren't Russian either, because when we left I heard one of them talking Afrikaans to the 'Gypsy' lady who told fortunes and sold tickets. And when Chad appeared, the acrobat put his arm around his shoulders and said,

'Howzit, *boet*?' Russians didn't say 'Howzit' even if they had learnt to speak Afrikaans. But the connection between Chad and the acrobat made him even more beautiful. It would be fun to live with Chad in the orphanage. Together we could sneak out and play at the circus and learn tricks from the people who worked there. Chad could teach me how to smoke and he'd put his arm around my shoulders.

Petrus said to my sister, 'Did you like that, Rachie?'

'Thanks, Petrus,' she said, 'that was fun.' But I could tell she didn't like it. For a moment I was proud of my sister. I was proud that she didn't like the circus and I was proud that she was polite to Petrus.

'Gosh,' Petrus said, 'did you see those ladies in the bikinis? Weren't they wonderful? I'm going to ask my mother if I can learn to ride horses too.'

'Jack!' someone shouted. I turned round.

'Hi, Chad,' I said.

'How you doin', china?'

'Good thanks. And you?'

'All right.' He stretched and as the singlet lifted to reveal his flat brown stomach I noticed a trail of downy golden hair that ran down from his navel. His eye caught mine and I blushed. He smiled, rubbed his stomach and pulled his shirt down.

'You go to the circus?' he asked.

'Ja.'

'I know that guy there.' He pointed to the acrobat.

'He's really good,' I said.

'Ja, he's going to teach me.'

'Cool.'

'He says I have the muscles to be an acrobat. You have a light for me?' he asked.

'Jack doesn't smoke,' Rachel said. 'Because smoking is bad for kids.'

'Shut up, Rachel,' I said.

'What about you?' Chad asked Petrus, but Petrus just shook his head. This good-looking boy from Mayfair had made him mute.

'Fuck,' Chad said, 'I'll just have to ask one of the Africans for a light. Catch you later, Jack.' He walked off.

'Who was that?' Petrus asked.

'A guy from school.'

'Are you friends?'

'Ja.'

'But he smokes.'

'So?'

'Do you play together at break time?'

'We don't *play*, Petrus. We hang out.'

'Is he your best friend?'

'We're good friends. Pretty good friends,' I lied. Next time, I thought, when Petrus and my sister weren't around, I would ask him if he wanted to come and swim in the pool; an orphan wouldn't turn that down.

'I've never seen him at your house,' Petrus said sulkily.

Susie pulled out a folded piece of paper from her apron.

'See what Lebo buy me for my birthday? It's a code 10. Do you know what a code 10 is, my baby? It's a truck licence.' Lebo was Susie's husband but they hadn't lived together for a long time. My mother said they were 'partially estranged', which meant that they were still friends but didn't want to see each other all the time, which explained why Lebo lived in Kabalazani.

'I laugh. I say to him, "why you buy me this thing? What I want with a truck licence?" He think I am going to drive

55

a truck? That one he is mad. I say I want a car licence but he say this one is same price.'

'But you can't drive,' I said.

'I will learn. Your mommy will teach me. Then I will take you to my village and I will show you where me and Michael grow up. Jack – you mustn't tell you father Lebo he buy me this thing. But Lebo he knows a lot of people. Whatever you want, you talk to Lebo. You mustn't worry. Lebo he will sort you out. He knows this one – he knows that one. I don't know where he meet this guys. Must be from the shebeen. You know, Jack – in Lesotho, Lebo is a prince. Did you know this thing?'

'Yes, Susie,' I said.

'He is part of the royal family. The King is his mother's cousin. So what you think? You think your Mama Susie is princess?'

'I guess so.'

'Ja, I am a princess but I wash your dirty socks. It's funny, neh?' She laughed. 'That guy at the driving school – what is his name? I can't remember – he is an Indian guy. If you see him you will think he is a black like me. His skin is black. But he has a big house. Jack – you must see – he has so many cars – big cars, expensive cars. He has a lot of money – Jack! He is an Indian guy but he's as rich as your daddy. The Indians are very clever. The Indians are like the whites. They make the good business. I say to Lebo he must make like this Indian guy and make a good business so I can retire. When you turn eighteen, Lebo he will take you to that guy, he will sort you out and get you a licence. If you want to drive a truck he will get you a code 10.'

My mother called Lebo a 'wheeler-dealer' even though he was a Zionist. The Zionist Christian Church took God very seriously. They didn't have any buildings and used to worship in the parks and baptise each other in streams and dams. 'The Zed-See-See,' Susie always said, 'are very, very strict.' Lebo used to do all sorts of things for Susie. I thought it very unbecoming for Lebo to be a wheeler-dealer, because he was a prince, even though being an African prince was really not the same as Charles and Diana. It's not like people had to say 'Your Royal Highness' or 'Your Majesty'. In Africa, you could be a prince and have a very ordinary job and your wife still had to work in people's houses. But it was also good to know that Lebo could sort out a licence, and I made a mental note of this. Lisa failed her licence three times before she passed and she later confessed that on her last attempt she cried in the car and the police cop put his arm around her and said, 'Ag, girlie, don't cry. Should we try that parallel park again? But then you must promise not to tell anyone.' Perhaps this was a bad idea because Lisa never learnt to park properly. When my father said, 'You have to *reverse* into a parallel park,' my sister said, 'That's the way *you* do it. I have my own way.' But if Lebo had connections this was good because my sister said parallel parking was the most difficult thing in the world and perhaps I'd inherited her deficiencies. It was OK for a girl to fail three times, but it was terrible for a boy.

I spent most summer afternoons in the swimming pool. Susie's son Percy had come to stay for a while and it spoilt things because invariably he would be sitting on the stoep, watching. I wished that Percy would go home to Kabalazani. It was embarrassing having him around. I had to be on my best behaviour. I could not be rude to Susie or ignore her in front of her son. I had to pretend that Susie was an adult like my parents. I had to be attentive

57

to the awkwardness of the situation. If not, I would be just like Petrus or his parents or my aunts and uncles. Nothing made them awkward. They were completely at ease with black people milling about doing their bidding. But black people did not seem to like me any better for my awkwardness. They did not appreciate that I found the situation embarrassing. At least Petrus and his parents and my aunts and uncles didn't pretend things weren't as they were.

Percy slept on Susie's settee, watched TV and disappeared in the evenings. My parents were tense about the arrangement. One could not be sure what he had seen or done. There was a battle going on. The blacks could not control their children and it was said they were doing murderous things on the streets of Soweto. He must have been about sixteen when he came to stay with us. He was a scrawny and sullen boy. He lived with Susie until he was three and then went to live with his grandmother in Kabalazani. Sometimes he would come to visit us for weekends or a few days in the holidays, but not often, and because he was a few years older than me, we were not friends. Susie's mother was old and not coping well. 'He's difficult that one,' Susie often said. Because of strikes and riots it seemed that schools were closed more often than they were open and so Percy and his friends caught taxis into Pretoria or Johannesburg to drink and party. Susie said, 'They are tsotsis, these kids. They are bad guys. I don't like this.' This sounded marvellous and frightening. Percy may have been five years older than me but I felt like I was much more than five years away from catching a taxi into Hillbrow or Marabastadt – surely a decade at least. Percy, it seemed to me, was like so many other young blacks, a man-boy. Although he was scrawny, he looked older than he was. However, it was not only the fact that

Percy was a black youth that made my parents uneasy, it was also something particular about the sullen and secretive Percy that stirred their unease.

It all became too much for Susie's mother when Percy packed his bags and said he was moving to Lesotho to stay with his father's family. Susie let it be known that he had very romantic notions about the Lesotho royals and that although there wasn't apartheid in Lesotho that hardly counted in its favour because there wasn't much of *anything* in Lesotho. Lesotho had mountains and funny woven hats and donkeys. 'South Africa is better than Lesotho,' Susie said. 'In Lesotho the people are real, *real* Africans. Me too – I am a real African but at least I can read. The people in Lesotho are very, very ignorant. They are nice people but, Jack, they know nothing. What Percy want to do? He want to be a herd boy? Ha ha ha! This one is too weak. What he know about the cattle? Nothing!'

'Maybe he can live with his dad,' I suggested.

'No – Lebo is very busy. He works late in Pretoria. He works there in the courthouse. And Percy he say he doesn't like his father. They argue all the time. I phone Lebo, I say he must talk to this boy, but Lebo say the boy is too cheeky, he doesn't listen. He say, "I can't raise a child." He say it's a woman's job to raise a child. I say to him, "This is *new* times. This is *modern* times." But he won't listen. You know, Jack, Percy's father is so strict. He's very, very strict that one. He is a Zionist. The Zionists, they don't like smoking. They don't like drinking. They are very strict. More strict than your daddy. More strict than your Ouma. More strict than Boers. And Percy, he doesn't like the Zionists. I like the Zionists but sometimes people can be too strict. Maybe someone likes to drink a beer. Your daddy, he likes to drink a beer, it's not the end of the world. That is why

Lebo doesn't like his family in Lesotho. Ha ha – he try – he say to them they must stop drinking. Jack – they get so angry. Ha ha.'

One night when it looked like Susie's mother was losing the battle, like Percy really was going to go on an adventure to Lesotho, she phoned and Susie raced to Kabalazani and brought him back to our house away from the tsotsis, and the drinking, away from Marabastadt, so that she could calm him down and give him time to think about what to do next. It was not, she reasoned, as if school mattered at this late stage. He would have to try again next year.

'I tell Percy he must be like you, Jack. I tell him you are a good boy. I say to him, "Jack goes to school, Percy. Jack he is going to do the matric. But you don't even have standard seven." Am I right, Jack? Yes, I am right. I *must* tell him these things. I tell him I have standard three. He must not be stupid like me. Percy is a very clever boy, but he is so lazy. You know, Jack, when I was young, I love to go to school. I love it so much. But now these kids in the townships – they are tsotsis. You know what a tsotsi is, Jack? A tsotsi is a very bad guy. These kids, they don't listen to what their mother tell them. They don't listen to what their father tell them. Their mothers and their fathers, they are right. You must get an education. Hey, Jack? You too, you must get the matric. You mustn't worry too much about the girlfriends. Percy, always he has *this* one, he has *that* one. He say to me, "But I love her, Mama." It is rubbish! Hey, Jack? But I tell him, Jack is a good boy. He is such a handsome boy. He doesn't worry about girls. Jack is going to do the matric.'

For Susie, a matric, the school-leaver's exam that enabled you to study at university, was a guarantee of a person's success in the world. It was the most important academic achievement and a testament of a person's good character. Susie invested it with an almost supernatural power. Once you had matriculated you were immune to the vicissitudes of an anarchic society. I was not sure whether these reported conversations with Percy were accurate, though I feared they were.

Sammy ran around the garden, excitedly barking and lapping at my feet.

'Go away, Sammy – stupid dog!' I picked up a tennis ball and threw it across the garden but he didn't take any interest. 'Why can't you be a normal dog?' He jumped up, put his paws on my chest and licked my face. 'Gross!'

Sammy's mother was a beautiful red-setter bitch and his father a nice enough, but not especially pedigreed, Labrador who'd managed to jump a six-foot fence. We loved Sammy too much, for he never outgrew his puppyish behaviour and would try to sit on your lap while you watched TV or crawl into bed with you and lay his head next to yours on the pillow. My father would take Sammy by the head, place his mouth on the dog's, and inflate his jowls like fleshy balloons. This would make Rachel laugh and she'd say, 'Daddy's kissing Sammy and blowing him up. Look – Daddy's blowing up Sammy.'

I sat on the pool ledge and dangled my feet in the water. It was still a little murky from the chlorine granules. We put in too much chlorine and acid. If the water didn't sting your eyes and your itchy bites, if you couldn't taste the chlorine, my mother was convinced it was dirty. She believed it was good to swim just after a dose of chlorine granules even though there were strict instructions on the packaging not to do so. When her children smelt of chlorine, my mother was happy.

Sammy sat next to me and licked my ear. When he was a few months old, my mother said, 'The dog needs a friend,' and we drove to the SPCA to buy him a mate. I fell in love with a forlorn-looking dog in cage A26. 'I've found our new dog,' I announced.

'No you haven't,' said Lisa.

'Let me see,' said Rachel.

We gathered in front of the cage. 'That is the ugliest dog I've ever seen in my life,' said Lisa.

'She's got stripes,' said Rachel, 'we can call her Stripy.'

'What do you think?' I asked my dad.

'Well, it's up to you kids,' he said.

'Jack,' Lisa said, 'why do you have to choose the ugliest dog in the world?'

'I like this dog. It's got character.'

A woman from the SPCA overheard the conversation and walked up to us.

'Ag, I'm so glad you like this dog. She's been here for months. We were just about to put her to sleep.' Lisa sighed. My father sighed. Rachel said, 'I like sleeping too.'

She was a brindled greyhound-like dog, but with none of its elegance. Her coarse hair was unpleasant to touch and her pointy ears folded over next to big mournful eyes that were too far apart. In polite circles, people might refer to her as a 'township' dog, for she was the type of dog you might see roaming the dusty streets of Alexandra or Soweto, but most people we knew would say, 'Hey – you got yourself a kaffir brak', and even people who would never otherwise use this word would call her a kaffir brak in the same way that they spoke about kaffir trees because they didn't know another word.

'Can we call her Stripy?' Rachel asked.

'No, Rachel, that's a stupid name.'

'Can we call her Spotty?'

'She doesn't even have spots, Rachel.'

'That dog should be pushing up the daisies,' Lisa said.

'Can we call her Daisy?' Rachel said.

But when Susie saw the dog she said, 'Mmm – she is very ugly. But I can trust. If you look in the dog's eyes you can see if you can trust. This one I can trust. Call it Thembisa – it means trust.'

The unexpected abundance of our home made Thembisa fat and lazy. Her body grew until the rolls of fat behind her head filled out and her neck was no longer distinguishable.

Now as Sammy galloped around the garden, Thembi lay on her back with her matchstick legs in the air. She looked dead. 'Thembi?' I said. She turned her head towards me to see if I was offering food. She moved so infrequently that the flies began to eat her ears. It was easy to love Sammy but it took effort to love a fat kaffir brak. That's why I lavished affection on her. I didn't want her to feel bad for being ugly and smelly. I didn't want her to know that I loved Sammy more. If I pretended to love Thembi, Lisa and my father could say, 'Well, at least *he* really loves that mutt of a dog,' and they'd think it had been worth saving her.

I was a natural swimmer, not so comfortable as the children who had grown up in Cape Town or Durban, who swam in the sea every day and had to contend with strong tides and rough waves. Instead, I had the confidence of one who had grown up playing in the chlorinated water of a private swimming pool, who cut through the water without splashing and revealed a degree of proficiency in all strokes, bar butterfly, which I could never master. I swam until I felt cold and then splashed water on to the slate-stone surround. Soon the water was warm as blood and I lay by the pool, breathing in the steam. Small pieces of black slate stuck to my cheek and left red indentations in my skin. The steam had a distinctive smell of hot stone, chlorine and urine. At the height of summer, the stone would quickly become too hot to lie on, and I would splash more water out of the pool to cool it down. Flies buzzed above me and I lay still, waiting for them to land on my back. I liked the gentle tickling sensation as they explored my skin, feasting on whatever it was the body secreted or shed to nourish them. All the air between my stomach and the slate-stone was squeezed out. I moved and the air seeping back into the small crack between the stone and my flesh made a gentle farting noise. I could not count the number of hours that my friends and I spent baking, facing one another, like lovers, conspiring about things to do to fill the summer days.

But lately Percy was always there, staring at me through two slits. I pretended to be asleep but I watched Percy. What was there to stop him from walking over and kicking me in the stomach or stabbing a knife into my back? What was there to stop Percy from dragging me into the swimming pool and drowning me? Did he not want to reclaim his mother from this boy who needed, demanded, two mothers? Why did all the black boys not reclaim their mothers? They would not have to kill all the whites; just the children, the first-born sons perhaps. That would be enough to paralyse the whites with grief so that they could take their mothers home. No matter what happened, would these boys not be forever crippled by this loathsome submission to it all? When I looked at Percy, I felt swell within me in equal measure contempt and guilt.

4

Fuck off and leave us alone

MY ENGLISH SCHOOL was not so very different from the Afrikaans school three blocks down the road. From Mondays to Thursdays morning assembly was held in the field. The teachers stood on the steps that led to the main school building and addressed the children below. Emmanuel had a mop of dark curly hair and was reputed to be the cleverest boy in our year. Secretly I thought Emmanuel almost but not quite as clever as me, though I never dissented publicly against everybody's estimation of Emmanuel as 'definitely the cleverest boy in school at the moment and possibly the cleverest boy ever'. His father was a scientist who invented explosives for Johannesburg's gold and platinum mines. The teachers were less fond than might be expected of the star pupil who won all the prizes, including *first place* in the Transvaal Science Olympiad for the 'promotion of natural sciences within the primary schools of the province', because Emmanuel was not sweet and demure, as the cleverest children ought to be. Many years later, my friends and I discovered to our dismay that

65

Emmanuel was the first to lose his virginity. He was working in a cabbage factory outside Liverpool and wrote to tell me he had slept with an Irish girl who had sex with many men. Working in the cabbage factory was unpleasant but necessary because only people who had worked in cabbage factories could read Brecht, Steinbeck and Beckett. I crumpled the letter and wished syphilis on him.

If ever a pupil was late for assembly, Mr Harrison would interrupt the announcement to cast his eyes on the offending pupil crossing the field and call out, 'Please don't rush on our account.' Fat Thomas Baird would break into an ungainly sprint, chubby thighs rubbing together. He'd place his index finger firmly on the bridge of his glasses to prevent them sliding down his nose and wobble, flushed and breathless, towards the assembled students. Thomas Baird was saved a cruel nickname by virtue of the fact that we were unfamiliar with *Lord of the Flies*. To adults, it must have seemed as if Piggy himself had been plucked from the jungle moments before the fateful blow and deposited on the playing fields of John Adams Primary.

There were many things we found funny about Thomas, other than his weight. His mother was a little bit famous for presenting a radio show called *Women's Hour* and notorious for telling us to speak properly. 'When you speak, you must enunciate your words. To *enunciate* means to speak clearly. Listen to the way Thomas speaks. He *enunciates* his words.' And indeed, Thomas did. He won a part in a television advert and was paid R300 for his efforts, a not inconsiderable sum, but it wasn't nearly enough to compensate him for the years of taunting he suffered in high school. Being obese was bad, being the South African Milky Bar Kid was far worse.

Jürgen Grossman was the clumsy son of German

immigrants. He was a head taller than the rest of us, with two shapeless tree trunks for legs. When Jürgen told me his father had cancer, I assured him that it was nothing to be concerned about – 'People get cancer all the time. It's like getting a bad cold' – but when we learnt that his father had died, I thought it would have been better to tell Jürgen what I suspected all along. Cancer is probably a lot worse than a cold. His father is going to die, I thought, and none of us are going to know what to say to him. It's going to be very embarrassing. When Jürgen returned to school he said, 'My father died,' to which I replied, 'Mrs Clarence told us.'

'He had cancer in his spine.'

'I didn't know people got cancer in the spine.'

'Neither did I,' he said before asking, 'Do you believe in heaven?'

And I said yes, because I was a polite child, though I wasn't sure. I wondered whether I would have to wear my school uniform at the funeral, but I wasn't invited, so it didn't matter. Dead father aside, Jürgen did small things that simply proved too tempting for eleven-year-old boys to ignore. He might, for instance, tuck a thick paperback novel into the back of his trousers during morning assembly. This would create a gap between the fabric and his pale, fatty flesh into which the person standing behind would drop little bits of whatever was to hand. If everything went to plan, Jürgen's attempt to extricate a dead cricket from his bottom might get him called out of morning assembly. If all the planets were in alignment, Mr Harrison might say, 'Jürgen, have you got worms?'

Aaron Schwartz was the only one of us to have entered puberty. During PT lessons we could not help but stare at him. We were curious about, and certainly envious of, his rapid metamorphosis. He stood tall, hairy and fecund among children. He was ashamed of his body and conscious of the leering eyes waiting to catch a glimpse of their future selves. I think he regarded his body as indecently premature, as if sitting at the dinner table he had inadvertently started his course before everyone else had been served. Of course, the rest of us thought this shyness ridiculous. If at the age of eleven *we* had been blessed with generously proportioned man dicks we would have strutted naked around the changing rooms, the playing fields, the corridors and the classrooms, calling out, 'Drink in my rugged manliness. Feed your hungry and desiring eyes.' But between my thighs and indeed between the thighs of the rest of the boys were small pink shrimps, which belied what was happening in our minds.

So it was that each of us had one distinguishing characteristic that stood in for all our other differences. Emmanuel was clever and Thomas was fat. Jürgen had a dead dad and Aaron a hairy willy. And me? Perhaps I was cruel. I dismissed this thought and decided that, if asked, my friends would agree that my distinguishing characteristic was that I was half English and half Afrikaans, that I could slip unnoticed between the two peoples like a spy.

I ended the moratorium on teasing Jürgen by saying, 'German salami smells like fart.' A piece of it had become lodged between Jürgen's yellow corncob teeth. It was surprising, after the initial shock, to see how quickly life returned to normal.

Assemblies concluded with the national anthem. In the spirit of bilingualism, it was sung in English one day and in Afrikaans the next.

From our plains where creaking wagons
cut their trails into the earth –
Calls the spirit of our Country,
of the land that gave us birth.
At thy call we shall not falter,
firm and steadfast we shall stand,
At thy will to live or perish,
O South Africa, dear land.

If you sat on the school roof, you might observe how
we left the assembly area, class by class. It must have looked
like a giant centipede disturbed, unwinding itself into the
bright morning; a *shongololo* of children, segmenting as it
travelled down the concrete passages. If you were higher
up, in a helicopter perhaps, you might see the same ritual
happening at the school down the road, and hundreds, even
thousands of times over in schools indistinguishable from
one another across a country inventing for itself a history
in which English people and Afrikaans people sat side by
side on ox-wagons cutting trails into an earth of gold and
diamonds, on a journey ordained by God.

This fantasy of English people and Afrikaans people
sitting side by side on ox-wagons might sound ridiculous,
and of course it is, especially in light of the Anglo-Boer
War and the concentration camps and *all that*, but in the
eighty or so years since the unpleasantness we seemed, by
and large, to have got over most of our differences.

There were some animosities that were passed down from
one generation to the next, which eventually found expression on the cricket and rugby fields. And in these battles,
unlike the actual war, there was no contest. The Afrikaners
wiped the floor with us. The Afrikaners were bigger and
stronger and more brutish. Prolonged exposure to

Afrikaans masculinity was, quite frankly, withering. Of course, one could point out that there were plenty of soft Afrikaans boys too – like young Petrus, who, even at the age of eleven, was quite evidently a *moffie*. But his *moffie*-ness was brought into such excruciatingly sharp relief precisely because he was an Afrikaner. Young Petrus seemed a much more likely product of my odd, soft family than that builder father and matronly mother. What was so striking about Petrus's *moffie*-ness was that his brother was the apotheosis of Afrikaner evolution, the product of five generations of blood and sweat and tears. He was heroically proportioned. Anton, not Petrus, was what nature selected to cross the mountains, fight the English, break the blacks and found a nation. After three hundred years of fighting and fucking, Anton was a little bit of human hardness that tore its way out of a meaty Afrikaner cunt. Anton was what nature intended; the indomitable spirit made flesh. So against Anton and his ilk, these hard boys, these Darwinian marvels, we did not fare well, and quite frankly, they scared the shit out of us on the playing fields. But other than that, the differences were mostly settled for our generation, making it pretty easy to buy into the fantasy of the founding of South Africa which included all sorts of ridiculous things, but none so holy as the ox-wagon.

We lined up outside our classrooms and waited for our teachers, who, in twos and threes, came strolling down the corridors. Thomas, who had just told us that his father smoked marijuana in the garden workshop, was indignant about our scandalised response.

'My father is an artist. That means he is different to other people. Artists are more enlightened,' Thomas said.

'Does your mother smoke dagga too?' I asked.

My friends burst out laughing and Thomas shook his head in dismay.

'I am a relative of John Logie Baird,' Emmanuel said, 'who invented the television. My husband and I smoke marijuana in the garden shed. It helps us enunciate our words.'

Thomas smiled and pushed his glasses to the bridge of his nose. On the subject of marijuana use, my grandmother, when she was still living in her own house, had said, 'In theory, marijuana is not much worse than a cigarette. But look at my gardener; he rakes the leaves in circles all day, he never actually picks them up. Either he has forgotten what he is supposed to do with them or he has just become lazy. It is not in the nature of black people to be lazy, but how could you forget to put the leaves in the bag? Black people are hard workers, *in theory* – though you have to keep an eye on them.' I didn't know whether Ouma was saying something about marijuana or the nature of black people, but her laissez-faire pronouncement revealed something reckless and unexpected about her personality. I hadn't known anyone else to say that marijuana was not much worse than cigarettes. Not even my sister.

Smiling and pushing his glasses to the bridge of his nose was what Thomas did whenever we teased him. He thought being a child unfortunate ('Thomas is an old soul,' his mother used to say) and was eagerly awaiting a time when being fat and speaking funny didn't matter as much as it did when you were eleven; a time perhaps when he might wear a waistcoat and bow tie. But when you started adding up all the little things that the universe did to Thomas Baird, you realised that there were more mean tricks than his fatness and his odd mother and his pot-smoking father.

The world was entering the golden age of computing, a

time when your parents' accretion of computing hardware helped determine your place within the social hierarchy of your peer group, and unfortunately for young Thomas Baird his radio-personality mother had barely reconciled herself to the arrival of *television* (in spite of her son's star turn, in spite of the fact even that she *was* a relative by marriage of John Logie Baird). Thomas spied an opportunity. His mother's reluctance to participate in the technological revolution was compromising him, educationally. How, he wanted to know, could he possibly be expected to keep up with his friends, let alone be competitive if he was unable to avail himself of the latest technology? Mrs Baird was distraught. Had she not done enough damage by allowing him to become so fat? It was true of course that Thomas spoke beautifully, as if he had been born and raised in England, but aided and abetted by technology, these philistines might overtake her son. And Mrs Baird always had the very best of intentions.

'My mother is going to buy me a computer,' he told us during break time. 'The very best.' And indeed Mrs Baird made good on her word. She gave him the very best, the most expensive, the most extravagant, the most sought after electric typewriter that money could buy. Oh the howls of derision that greeted the arrival of his brand-new Olivetti. If ever we needed evidence that the universe was a mean son of a bitch (apart, of course, from the millions of people suffering horribly under our tyrannical rule), then you only needed to look at the tragic life of Thomas Baird.

Marietta Hennings stubbed out her cigarette on the balcony handrail and flicked the butt over the school fence. She waited for us to pick up our bags and fall quiet. Then, with a nod of her head, first the girls then the boys filed into class. We took our seats and started chatting. She gazed out of the window and let her focus soften as the noise washed over her. She only permitted herself a few moments of surrender. We were approaching adolescence. I think she must have seen the adoration seeping out of us and the first traces of sullenness creeping in. It would not be long before this sullenness would swell and erupt.

Marietta Hennings had a tight red perm, small hard eyes and thin lips. Her skirts and dresses always came down to the knee to reveal her slim and muscular calves, of which she was very proud. Mrs Hennings had been the hundred-metre hurdle champion at Stellenbosch University. There was a rumour that, had South Africa not been banned from it, Mrs Hennings would have been a real medal prospect at the Munich Olympic Games in 1972. But it was too late for her and she would have to make her mark on the world in an altogether more modest way.

Mrs Hennings was our history teacher and her zeal for the subject was evidenced by the impassioned lessons she prepared for her assembled eleven-year-olds.

'When Piet Retief and the Boers were in the hut, Dingane shouted, "Kill the wizards," and all the Zulu soldiers set upon them and stabbed them with their *iklwas*,' she said in such a way that the historical importance of this event could not be lost on us. 'They stabbed them with their *iklwas*,' she said while pounding her fist into her delicate hand. 'What, class, is an *iklwa*?'

'A short stabbing spear,' we chorused.

'That is correct. The *iklwa* is the short stabbing spear, invented by Shaka Zulu, the greatest of the Zulu chiefs. Shaka Zulu, brother of Dingane; Dingane, traitor of the

Zulus, betrayer of the Boers. What, class, is the name of the long throwing spear?'

'The *assegai*,' we said.

'That is right. The *assegai* is the long throwing spear; traditionally the weapon of choice, but no good for stabbing people in huts.'

Because Mrs Hennings was the severest of the teachers, because none of us, even those who lived in suburbs like Brixton and Mayfair, would 'give her lip', and because Mrs Hennings was Afrikaans, she was the teacher designated to deal with problem girls. What happened behind closed doors within the history classroom during break times or after school would only ever be known to those who emerged with puffy eyes, newly contrite and demure as was befitting of little girls in a primary school. She was not like some of the other Afrikaans teachers. She did not confuse her 'is's' and 'are's', nor did she raise her voice. The respect she commanded was absolute and only the most foolish of children would dare to test her patience.

Mrs Hennings walked towards Aaron and perched on the end of his desk like an eagle, red talons splayed on either side of her small but powerful frame.

'The Day of the Vow is the most important day in our history,' she said, pausing between sentences to give her words air, to allow them to settle on the heads of her young and impressionable students. 'We are remembering a historical event but also praising God for His mercy. The Day of the Vow is when history and God come together. This reminds us that it is God, not man, who decides what happens in the world. Now, complete your worksheets and paste them into your history books. When you are done, you may use your pencils to colour in the scene at the

74

bottom of the page. As you can see, it depicts the moment that Piet Retief realises that he has been betrayed. He is standing ready to defend his men, though he knows this is a battle he can never win. Piet Retief was a brave man. South Africa has many brave ancestors.'

We looked at our photocopied sheets. The lines contained a series of leading omissions. The steady accumulation of omissions marked our progress through the schooling system. By the time we reached matric, we would be faced only with a blank sheet of paper.

The Voortrekkers and the Day of the Vow

The Groot Trek began in 1835 when Piet Retief and other Boers decided to leave the Cape because of the wars with the Xhosas and the (*Emancipation Act*). They went to Natal and made a deal with (*Dingane*), King of the Zulus, but he set a trap and killed them. The Boers were (*betrayed*) by the Zulus. Then the Zulus ran all day and all (*night*) until they found the (*trekker*) party. The Zulus killed (*530*) Boers. The Afrikaners were very angry with Dingane so they swore a vow with (*God*). On (*16 December*) the Boers fought another war with the Zulus. The Zulus are a (*proud*) nation. They have spears and shields and are (*fierce*) in battle. The Boers killed so many Zulus that the rivers ran red with (*blood*). That's why the war is called (*Blood River*). Today we celebrate this victory. It is known as the (*Day*) of the (*Vow*).

As we went to work on our sheets, Mrs Hennings walked up and down the rows, occasionally leaning over our shoulders, so close that you could feel her breath on your neck. It would not do to be 'clever' when completing these sheets, for instance writing that the Boers had been 'fooled' rather than 'betrayed'. Mrs Hennings was as sensitive to our choice of words as our English teacher.

'Fooled,' she said coolly to Emmanuel, 'is not correct. If I invite you into my classroom and stab you with my scissors, would the police tell your parents that you had been fooled?'

She walked towards the window, arms folded, and stared at the fields where the ground staff were retouching the boundary lines. She looked pensive. I wondered whether she was thinking about athletics or the Day of the Vow. Like Good Friday, the Day of the Vow was a very important day in South Africa. God answered the Boer prayers and killed three thousand Zulus. That's why Afrikaners said that God was on their side. That's why Afrikaners thought God would smite the Russians. No doubt Mrs Hennings thought so too.

Sometimes Mrs Hennings argued with Jenny Barnard, the *English* history teacher. For instance, when teaching the Anglo-Boer War Mrs Hennings insisted on including a picture of Lizzie van Zyl, an emaciated child in a British concentration camp. Jenny Barnard considered the picture 'lurid' and instructed her pupils to paste over it with a blank sheet of paper. She felt this image spoilt the attractive exercise books which we would spend the year producing. South African history should be brought to life with a quality tin of Faber-Castell and it wasn't right to colour in dead Afrikaans kids. There could be no doubt that some unpleasant incidents were included in the curriculum, but teachers did not give the children drawings of fields littered with Zulu corpses. But as eleven-year-olds, even as *English* eleven-year-olds, we would have had Mrs Hennings over Mrs Barnard any day.

We would have had Mrs Hennings over any other teacher because Mrs Hennings had balls, great big brass balls which hung just above her nicely proportioned calves, clanging together, ringing in the arrival of someone who mattered, who had spine, someone who was worth giving a fuck about.

'Jürgen, why do you think there is a picture of Wolraad Woltemade on the King's Medal for Bravery?' Mrs Hennings asked.

'Because he drowned, Miss,' Jürgen responded.

'Drowning is not heroic, Jürgen. Drowning is easily achieved. Every year dozens of people drown. That does not make them heroes. More often it makes them fools.'

'Because he saved people, Miss,' Jürgen tried again.

'Because, Jürgen, he gave up his life to save others. Like you, Jürgen, Wolraad was also German. He came to South Africa to escape the decadence of Europe. We are the New World. Europe is the Old World. On the morning of the first of June 1773, a sailing ship was driven ashore by a terrible gale. It was bitterly cold and the sea was so rough that the ship was breaking up as the waves crashed against it. Some of the sailors attempted to swim to shore, but the current was so strong that they were swept out into the ocean and drowned. Wolraad Woltemade mounted his horse and galloped into the ocean. As he reached the ship he called for the men to jump into the sea. They grabbed the horse's tail and were dragged to shore. Seven times, Wolraad rode into the sea and seven times he returned. Seven times he plunged into the icy blackness and seven times he saved two men. How many men did Wolraad save, children?'

'Fourteen,' the class responded.

'Fourteen men,' she said. '"They that go down to the sea in ships, that do business in great waters; These see the works of the Lord, and His wonders in the deep."'

For Marietta Hennings, history was a detailed appendix to the Bible, a simple and unambiguous battle between the righteous and the wicked, the brave and cowardly, the sacred and the profane. History was the progression to the day when farm workers would pick up their scythes and say, 'Let's march to the cities and put these to better use,' their way lit by exploding airliners, the fireworks of liberation; the maids singing and dancing in the streets of Johannesburg, for who would vacuum during the Second Coming?

'"These see the works of the Lord, and His wonders in the deep,"' she said in her sonorous tones that filled the classroom, and I felt a chill in my spine, and an awe for the magnificent cruelty of God's insouciance.

'But the eighth time would be his last. As Wolraad approached the ship, it began to break apart and six men dove into the water, knowing that this would be their only chance of salvation. All six men grabbed Wolraad and his horse. They were dragged beneath the waves and drowned.'

Mrs Hennings stood, taut as a bow, with muscular thighs and small hard eyes, staring at us, willing us to feel a cold and salty death for ourselves.

Without these lessons, history would have become nothing but an unflattering portrait of the founding fathers: When the British took the Cape, the Afrikaners said, 'To hell with them, Africa is big – *ons gaan trek* [we're going to move],' and they packed their bags and crossed the mountains. And when the British came again, they said, 'To hell with you – *ons gaan baklei* [we're going to fight],' and they fought two long wars. And so it went on, children. What was the rallying cry of the Afrikaner? Fuck off and leave us alone, Miss. That's right, children, fuck off and leave us alone.

5

The Steyn family

EVEN IN 1989, ten rand didn't go very far. You could, *theoretically*, go to the movies four times. But then only if you didn't buy anything to eat or drink. And the chances were pretty good that you'd buy a grape-flavoured Slush Puppie. And that cost nearly as much as your movie ticket. But you'd spend the extra two rand, and seeing as you had already spent four fifty, you might as well buy a chocolate to round the afternoon's entertainment up to five rand, which meant that even though *in theory* you could go to the movies four times, I don't think there was a single month in my childhood that I actually managed it.

Or, you might spend your whole allowance on a He-Man doll, though we never called them dolls – they were just He-Mans, as in, 'Ma – can I buy myself a He-Man?' The title character's name stood in for the complete set of figures, of which there were sufficient in number to bank-rupt a family should they give in to a child's every whim. I don't recall anyone mentioning the peculiar tautology. Perhaps She-Man was inconceivable, or we just accepted that masculinity redoubled was really the only way to express it properly. Whatever the case, a He-Man would set you back for the month because they were at least ten rand and every time the president said something that upset people they would cost even more. Some kid in our class who went away on holiday to America said that no one there played with He-Mans any more and they weren't cool but it turned out he didn't actually go to America, he went to Canada, and everyone knew that Canada was most assuredly *not* America because they were almost communists. So it made sense that they didn't play with He-Mans because everyone knew communists didn't have toys. They played with pieces of wood and the bones of Christian children. At least this is what we told ourselves because we loved He-Mans very much and America was the great arbiter of coolness because they made everything we cared about and desired. If someone had said to us that *E.T.* or *The Goonies* was based on a true story, we would have believed it without question, because America was a place where anything could happen – and frequently did. And, importantly, our parents said that America was still friends with us, not best friends, but good friends because they chose President Bush instead of Dukakis. He had a good name, I thought, Dukakis. It sounded like carcass. When I asked my parents who they wanted to win the election they said, 'Well, it will be good if Dukakis wins but it might be a little tricky for a while.' This was not a satisfactory answer. People were good or bad and if they wanted Dukakis to win they should have said so and not muddied things by saying, 'It might be a little tricky.' Deep down, maybe they wanted Bush to win because my parents hated anything tricky.

Whatever the Americans really thought about He-Mans, the *suggestion* that a He-Man wasn't cool was enough to make us wonder a little. Perhaps there was something a bit off about playing with a man in his underwear with really big muscles, nearly as big as boobs, but definitely no willy. Him being willy-less, well, it was reassuring, there was nothing sexual about it, but then again, he didn't have a dick, not even a teeny little *tottie* like a nursery-school kid.

Some children got twenty rand pocket money. That didn't mean their parents were rich, it meant they didn't know how to raise their children. Even if you were rich everyone knew you should give children only ten rand a month. Ten rand was sufficient, not excessive. Ten rand could buy you the small luxuries that every child was entitled to, but still leave you unsatisfied so that you would remain in thrall to the power and the delights of money, in no doubt that it was worth pursuing, even at high cost to yourself or others. So because the arbiters of cool traded in a foreign currency and because our inept government could only be relied upon to make the trappings of cool more and more expensive, Petrus and I were always looking for easy ways to make extra cash, which is how I found myself outside the OK Bazaar on a hot afternoon. I watched as Petrus approached an elderly lady walking out the shop. 'Hello, Tannie,' he said to her. 'Those bags look heavy – can I help you with them?'

'Ag, thank you, my child, please take this one.'

'Sure, Tannie,' he said, taking the bag. 'I really like Tannie's dress. Did Tannie buy the dress at Edgars?'

'No, I made it myself.'

'Really, Tannie? It's so beautiful. Where did you get the material?'

'At the Indian Plaza.'

'Really, Tannie? My ma says the Indian Plaza has all the

best material. And my sister says that real designers don't say "material" they say "fabric". But Tannie must watch out because the *koelies* will short-change you when you're not looking. That's what my ma says.'

She laughed. 'Here's my Toyota.' Petrus helped pack the groceries in the boot and received fifty cents for his efforts. 'You see,' he said as he sauntered back, 'it's so easy. You mustn't ask for money or anything. And you must never ask ooms – only ladies. You just say, 'Tannie, can I help you?' and then if they say yes you chat to them and say nice things and then sometimes they give you money.'

'What did you talk about?'

'The Indian Plaza.'

'The Indian Plaza? I don't know anything about the Indian Plaza.'

'Have you been there?'

'Ja.'

'Isn't it wonderful? When we were making the dress for my sister's matric dance we went to the Indian Plaza. They have material from all over the world. And the Indians who work in the shops are very nice even though they are crooks and *koelies* – but they know everything about materials and where they come from. My ma won't let me eat the nigger balls from the machine. I love nigger balls – isn't it clever how they change colour when you suck them? But you can see in the machine that there are dead flies in there and anyway everyone knows that the *koelies* like to spit on the nigger balls in case the white people eat them. Then you'll get *koelie* cooties. They have sequins and buttons and lace and everything. I said to my mom when I grow up I want to work in the Indian Plaza and she said I was being stupid. And then I said I wanted to work for South African Airways and then she said maybe working at the Indian Plaza wasn't a bad idea.'

He pointed to a woman leaving the store. 'There's a tannie with a lot of bags.' I walked up to her. 'Tannie looks tired. Can I help Tannie carry the bags?'

'I suppose,' she said. We walked to her car and though she didn't seem very friendly I tried to follow Petrus's advice.

'Did Tannie buy that dress from the Indian Plaza?'

'What?' she said.

'Did Tannie buy the dress from the Indian Plaza?' I asked again, smiling. She snatched the bag out of my hand. 'You're a very rude child. Go away.' Petrus saw this and hurried over. 'What happened?' he asked.

'She said I was rude.'

'Did you ask for money? You must never ask for money.'

'No – I said what you told me.'

'What?'

'I asked if she bought her dress from the Indian Plaza.' Petrus started giggling. A lot of the time Petrus irritated me. I was smarter than he was but he often acted like I was ignorant or, worse, like I was gauche and unsophisticated – which I was, but no more than he was. 'Only maids buy their clothes from the Indian Plaza.'

'But you said –'

'Material. White people buy material from the Indian Plaza. Never clothes. Only black people buy clothes from the Indian Plaza, unless you buy the one with the crocodile, but I think that's only for men. I'm not sure. Did her dress have a crocodile on it?' he asked.

'I don't know what you're talking about.'

'Probably not. She didn't look like she could afford crocodile dresses. Maybe you shouldn't talk to the tannies. Just help carry the bags and keep quiet.'

I punched him on his arm.

'What was that for?' he whined.

'For being an asshole,' I said. He gave me a painful knuckle punch. I forgot sometimes that, for a *moffie*, Petrus could be quite tough. He might know where white ladies do, and more importantly do not, buy their clothes but he also had an older brother who was built like a brick shithouse, with thick rippling muscles and a big cock (I'd seen him take a leak in the garden) and who definitely wasn't a virgin – so no matter how soft Petrus was, some of this invariably rubbed off on him and little bursts of toughness, of his street smarts (like the knuckle trick), would take me by surprise and make me jealous that I didn't have an older brother because really, in the end, there was no hope for Petrus.

In two hours Petrus made nine rand in tips, and though I didn't fare as well, it was easy money. The only time we made more money was when we sold his mother's clothes at our improvised jumble sale. Petrus had even made a cardboard sign that read 'JUMBLE SALE – CHEAP CHEAP!' The maids walking down the road to catch taxis on Barry Herzog Avenue bought everything and we ended the day with fistfuls of cash. At one point, Petrus, so excited by the business of business, shouted, 'Hurry – we're running out of stock! We're running out of stock!' and I replied, 'What's stock?' and he said, 'Clothes! Go to my ma's room and get some more clothes!' – so I grabbed what I could and flung it on the pavement. It was a disaster. When Tannie Vera found out what had happened she called my parents and I got a hiding from my father and Petrus got a hiding from Oom Frik and we had to give all the money back which was unjust because having got hidings we had *earned* that money. So making money at the OK Bazaar was good. It was much safer than selling

Tannie Vera's clothes, which, it turned out, was neither safe nor profitable.

As Petrus was about to approach another customer I noticed Percy waiting in line at one of the tills.

'Petrus,' I said, 'stop.'

'Why?'

'Percy is over there.'

'Who?'

'Percy – Susie's son.'

'Oh ja. So what?'

'He'll tell Susie.'

'So?'

'She'll tell my mother.'

'You think so?'

'Ja.'

'Why does Susie tell your ma everything? Will she give you a hiding?'

'Ja.'

'Or your father? Do you think your father will give you a hiding?'

'One of them will,' I said.

'Do you think he saw us when he went in?'

'I don't know.'

'You should talk to him.'

'What?'

'Go and talk to him. Tell him he mustn't tell Susie.'

'Are you crazy?'

'Give him two rand.'

'What?'

'Give him two rand.'

'I'm not giving him two rand. He didn't carry any groceries. I only made four rand.'

'But what if *your* mother tells *my* mother?' Petrus said.

'She won't.'

'But what if she does? My mother says I act like a poor white. When she saw Pierre helping the tannies like we are she said he was acting like a poor white and that it was disgusting.'

'She won't do anything.'

'She will – remember the jumble sale?'

'It was *your* mother. *Your* mother called my mother – and I got a hiding.'

'I got a hiding too,' he said a little hurt. 'If you don't talk to him I won't show you the book.'

'What?' I said.

'If you don't talk to him I won't show you the book.' Petrus had discovered a sex book in his mother's bedroom and had promised to show it to me that afternoon. It was very unfair of Petrus to blackmail me in this way because he could use our swimming pool whenever he wanted and he was allowed to eat as much cheese from our fridge as he wanted and Petrus could eat a lot of cheese. For Petrus to threaten me in this way must have meant he was desperate to protect this racket he had going outside the local grocery store. It wasn't the hiding he feared – it was the certainty that he would be expressly forbidden from doing it again, and to do something that his mother had expressly forbidden him from doing didn't bear thinking about. If Jesus Christ himself had come down from heaven and expressly forbidden Petrus from doing something it wouldn't hold as much weight.

'That's not fair, Petrus, you promised.'

'Just talk to him.'

Percy walked out the store carrying three shopping bags.

'Hi, Percy,' I said as I walked alongside.

'Hello.'

'It's hot today, huh?'

'Ja.'

'Are those Susie's groceries?'

'For your mother.'

'Oh,' I said. 'She could have sent me. I mean, Susie could have sent me.' He didn't say anything. We crossed the road together. Petrus trailed behind.

'Percy, please don't tell Susie about –' I trailed off.

'About what?'

'Oh . . . nothing. I mean – just don't tell Susie we were here. I was supposed to clean my room. I wasn't supposed to come out today.'

'You mean about your business,' he said. It came out as a sneer. Your beez-nus.

'It's not a business.'

'What you want money for? Do your mommy and daddy not give you money?'

'Of course – they give me pocket money,' I said, indignant.

'So I can't get a job, but you want money to buy more toys.'

This was very unfair of Percy. Susie was almost like my mother, which meant we were like brothers. And although he was sixteen and although he'd probably already had sex with girls it wasn't fair to make me sound like such a kid. It was true of course that I didn't really like Percy and that I resented him being there and that I was really desperate for him to leave so that I could have Susie to myself but I had never been openly hostile to him. I had always been polite.

'Well, Percy,' I said, 'maybe you shouldn't try and find a job. Maybe you should stay in school so that you can get a matric. If you get a matric you could get a good job. You could even go to Vista University. That's what Susie says.'

'Jack,' he said, 'go, or I will hit you.'

I was embarrassed. It was cruel to humiliate Percy. And we weren't really like brothers at all. Susie might have been like my mother, but he wasn't like my mother's son. He had to share Susie with me but I didn't have to share my mother with him. And though I didn't know for sure, I suspected Percy disliked me as much as I disliked him. I didn't think for a moment he would hit me, but I knew he wanted to. I wished he would hit me. Then we could be even. That would take back the horrible things I'd just said to him. I didn't move and he carried on walking. Petrus came running up to me.

'Did you give him the money?'

'No.'

'Is he going to tell Susie?'

'I don't know.'

'If he tells Susie I won't show you the book.'

'Fine. Don't. But then you can never come to my house again and never swim in my pool.'

'Ag – don't be like that. I was just joking.'

'Let's go now.'

'But my ma is there.'

'I don't care.'

'OK – but I have to feed my silkworms.'

Percy never did tell Susie. Susie would have told my mother and my mother *would* have given me a hiding.

The old yellow Land Rover was parked underneath the mulberry tree. Its dented bonnet and roof were covered in purple stains and bird droppings. Anton's brown legs poked out from beneath the car. He was wearing a pair of blue plastic flip-flops – the kind sold on Durban's beach-front – some shorts and a white singlet, the front of which was stained with sweat. He was stocky with a tuft of chest hair just visible above the neckline. Anton was twenty-four and had been discharged from the army. He cuffed me around the back of the neck and asked, 'How you doin', my china?'

His cheerful disposition and brilliant-blue eyes made it hard for me to believe that Anton had shot the neighbour's dog in a mad rage. It was a very small dog and in my mind a larger breed would have made the act less excessive. But about these things people said, 'Ag, you must understand, he's a little *bosbefok*' – bushfucked – 'he needs some time to settle down.'

Everyone knew that South Africa had been waging a war of sorts. The government claimed that South Africa was protecting the border between South West Africa and Angola, but my parents had explained that the situation was complicated. In the main, South Africa was helping a man by the name of Jonas Savimbi, the leader of UNITA, who were waging a war against the communist MPLA. Also in the mix were Cubans sent by a man called Castro. If the government was to be believed, Castro was the most evil man on the planet. I could not help but like Savimbi even though my parents had told me that he was a megalomaniac (at the time, my favourite word). Savimbi wore an army uniform with a red beret. The reporter from the South African Broadcasting Corporation would walk around the bush camp and say, 'As you can see, Jamba, the headquarters of UNITA, is a well-equipped military facility. Although conditions in Angola are hard, morale remains high as UNITA is determined to vanquish the communist MPLA. Earlier today, I spoke to Dr Jonas Savimbi about UNITA's struggle for the people of Angola.'

Savimbi had a large head with eyes that were set

abnormally far apart. His fleshy nose, flared nostrils, meaty hands and the entourage of soldiers armed with automatic weapons made him look like the most dangerous and powerful man in the world. Secretly I was rooting for Savimbi. I thought Savimbi would make a fine president for Angola, which, as far as I could tell, didn't have one. And Angola was a fine country to be president of. It had so many diamonds that land was covered with cement to prevent people from digging them up. Patrolling the area were guards who would shoot on sight, and vicious dogs who would tear you to pieces. I often thought about Angola: a vast cement wilderness and in the distance a pack of dogs, whipped into a salivating, snarling frenzy by an umbrella-wielding silhouette on the horizon. The dogs set upon me as I desperately try to steal a diamond half encased in cement. They tear open my aorta. Blood runs down my arm and pools around the glinting stone set between thumb, index and middle finger. My Chinese neighbour descends the cement dune, back arched, in small and graceful steps, shielding her face from the sun with her black umbrella. She leans across my body and wags a finger in my face.

'Communist diamonds! *Chinese* diamonds!'

Even though South Africa had indisputably been at war, whatever pathology lurked within Anton could not be ascribed to his national service. Five years previously he found himself in Voortrekkerhoogte (the army base in Pretoria), clad in nothing more than his underwear under the hot Pretoria sun. An army doctor placed a stethoscope on his chest and informed Anton that he had a heart murmur. The doctor removed the lid of his black marker and scrawled 'H4C4' across his left shoulder blade: Health 4, Condition 4. 'H4 fucked up' was the next best thing to being declared unfit for military service. Upon hearing that his son would spend the next two years in Lohatla, drinking tea and eating sandwiches while processing the salaries of men who were dying on the border, his father said, 'A murmur? What are you, a *moffie*?' to which Tannie Vera responded, 'Ag, don't be ridiculous Frik, the boy has a heart condition.'

Aside from the indignity of being designated an H4C4, Anton's military service caused him no trauma and should not have been submitted in mitigation of his crime. But neither Petrus nor I knew about this at the time and we accepted that he was bushfucked and should be forgiven the slaughter of what was, in any event, a disagreeable poodle that did bark in the small hours of the morning.

Anton walked around to the front of the car and peered at the engine.

'You boys come to pick leaves?' he asked.

'Ja,' we answered.

'You can stand on the roof if you like.'

'Really?' we asked.

'That's what a Land Rover is built for, man.'

We clambered on to the roof of the cab, picked leaves and stuffed them into two plastic shopping bags.

'My sister says if you feed silkworms lettuce leaves they spin pink silk instead of yellow. But my mother won't buy lettuce leaves because she says it's too expensive.'

I did not respond. I was embarrassed that Petrus had started talking about pink silk in front of his brother. He might have thought that I was also interested in where to go on holiday, the most fashionable colours of the season or how to serve tea in first class aboard South African Airways.

'It would be nice,' Petrus continued. 'My mother says

93

that silk is the most expensive material in the world. Last year when the moths came out I tried to pull the silk off the cocoons but it kept on breaking.'

Silkworms were a favourite pet every summer. They were not creepy like spiders and they didn't have the unpleasant odour of *shongololos*, the large black millipedes that children often played with. I liked their soft velvety bodies and their thick black stripes. You could deposit a heap of leaves in their box and within hours they had munched through them, leaving only serrated trails of their gluttony. After a few weeks, all that remained were springy yellow cocoons lashed with strings of silk to the side of a shoebox. When my mother tired of the silkworms she said the time had come to set them free. 'Those poor little worms,' she said. 'How would you like to be kept in a box?' I placed each delicate worm on its own leaf and wished it luck with its new life in our back garden. My mother said it was just terribly bad luck that a swarm of passing birds happened to discover this unnatural and defenceless abundance; all I could do was bear witness to the unfolding horror.

'Can you guys see into the neighbours' garden?' Anton asked.

'Yes,' I said.

'When I was a kid we used to sit in the tree and watch them have parties under the *lapa*. They have *lekker* parties next door. You guys should watch – sometimes the ladies take off their bikini tops. Have you guys got girlfriends yet?'

'No.'

He opened a beer and the foam ran over the side of the can.

'*Fok!*' he said, as he held it away from his body. The beer dripped into the pulp of mulberries and foamed on the ground. He held the can to his mouth, slurped the foam off the top and placed it on the roof of the cab before wiping his hands on his shorts and reaching into his pocket for cigarettes. I noticed that Anton, like my father, squinted whenever he lit a cigarette, shook the match to put out the flame and tilted his head back to exhale as he flicked the spent match to the ground. This was very manly and I resolved to do the same thing when I started smoking at fourteen. Fourteen was a good age to start smoking – an acceptable adolescent rebellion – before this was white trash.

The kitchen door swung open and Tannie Vera walked out holding a plastic container filled with birdseed, which she scattered on the grass in front of the stoep.

'*Kom kiep kiep kiep!*' she called out as the chickens, half running, half flying, raced towards her. '*Kom kiep kiep kiep!*'

Tannie Vera's dress ended just below her knee to reveal dark blue veins that twisted into angry knots on the back of her calves. She peered at the chickens over the tops of her bifocals that were attached to a plaited grey cord at either end. One of the chickens wandered into the entrance of the servant's quarters. Letsatsi sat on the bed polishing her shoes. Hanging from the cupboard behind her was a town outfit: a long dark skirt, a purple blouse and a printed jacket. From the top of the Land Rover, three independent lives unfolded, like pools of oil, intersecting at the circumferences; the tools scattered in the garden, the door of the room flung open to let in the summer breeze, the chickens wandering away from the kitchen. Around every human being were little ripples of activity that spread a few feet around them, mixing with the ripples of another. And I, standing on the roof of the Land Rover, standing absolutely still, thought myself detached from all this, thought myself blessed with a special acuity.

'Petrus, have you finished your chores?' Tannie Vera shouted.

'No, Ma,' he said.

'Well, come down and finish your chores. Jack can sit with me in the kitchen.'

Tannie Vera did not like me. She thought me a bad influence. Mostly she spoke English to me, which made her seem cool and disapproving. But the feeling was mutual. The Steyn household, as measured against my own, was wanting in a number of respects. In the television room they had upholstered wooden settees and in their lounge, reserved for guests and visits from the minister, light grey leather recliners. There were patterns on the carpet and clear vinyl runners in the passage. Mr and Mrs Steyn had five children, which was too many. In the garage were two large chest freezers, one for the sheep bought from a local farm and the other for the spoils of game-hunting. The family used the word 'bantu' for blacks. They took tortoises from the veld and kept them in the backyard. And though Letsatsi was a bad-tempered woman who hardly spoke to me, I disapproved of her accommodation and her dented zinc bath.

'Would you like a glass of Oros?' she asked.

'No thank you.'

Their juice made me wheeze because it contained enough sulphur dioxide to make an elephant asthmatic. It is testament to the stupidity of children and cheapness of adults that people, especially Tannie Vera, kept on buying this stuff by the gallon even though the sight of children lying by the poolside, struggling to breathe, was not uncommon. Tannie Vera would peer at me over the top of her bifocals and ask, 'Are you feeling OK, Jack?' and I would nod, not saying a word for fear that it would bring on a coughing fit. I knew she disapproved of my wheezing. She thought it the affectation of an unmannered English boy. She turned to Letsatsi.

'The *baas* is going to do some work on the house this weekend.'

'Yes, *missies* – you tell me.'

'Is there anything in your room that is broken?'

'No, *missies*.'

'Are you sure, Letsatsi? We must fix these things.'

Letsatsi picked up the diced carrots and put them into a large pot of boiling water.

'The toilet seat is cracked.'

Tannie Vera snapped, 'Did you break the toilet seat again? I got you a new one last year.'

'The year before.'

'You think money falls from the sky?'

Letsatsi picked up the chopping board and took it to the sink.

'Look at me when I am talking to you, Letsatsi. You know why that toilet seat is broken? Because of your fat sister. How do your people say, huh? *Stutla*. Your sister is very *stutla*.'

'It's not my sister.'

'Letsatsi, it's your sister. You must tell her not to sit on the toilet. She must stand a bit – over the toilet – like she's going in the bush, neh? How long has it been broken?'

Letsatsi shook her head.

'Maybe one year.'

'Why didn't you tell me?'

'It's the plastic. It cracks.'

'Are you saying I buy you a cheap toilet?

'No, *missies*.'

'You think all white people are rich? You think I can afford to put a porcelain toilet into the servant's quarters? Where do you think the money is going to come from? Mmmm?'

'I need to fold the washing.'

'I suppose I will finish this all myself.'

Letsatsi washed her hands and walked out.

'She gets in a real huff,' said Tannie Vera.

I squirmed and wondered why Letsatsi made life so difficult for herself. Surely it would've been easy to placate this woman? I sat at the kitchen table and said nothing. Tannie Vera was in a bad mood again. She always seemed to be in a temper. I wanted to open the door and let in some fresh air to dilute the thick suffocating smell of the mutton.

Susie loathed Tannie Vera. Word had spread across the six-foot fences and walls of Linden. Housekeeper spoke to housekeeper and gardener spoke to gardener. Letsatsi confided in Puleng, who spoke to Lefu, who wandered down the street to number 67, where Siphiwe worked, who spoke to everyone including Sophie, the old Zulu who worked next door to us and delivered to an enraptured Susie daily instalments about the goings-on in the Steyn household.

'That woman, Jack, she is a bitch. Petrus he is a nice boy. I know he's your friend. I like this one. Even if he eat all the cheese. Yes, I see him. That boy he eat so much cheese. But his mother – she is not a nice lady, Jack. You know her?'

'Yes,' I said, 'I know her.'

'Your mommy and your daddy – are they friends with this lady?'

'No, not really.'

'Yes – this is right. That lady she doesn't like the black people. She must respect. Don't you think? She must respect. So what? She is white. She is a human being. I am a human being. That is what is important. Petrus is a nice boy. He respect. Maybe he's a bit like a girl. He talk like girl. But I like him, even if he's a bit . . . funny. I can see he like to dress nice.' I giggled a little. 'Yes – I see. I have eyes. I see Petrus he like the nice shoes. He come to me the other day, Jack, I laugh, he say, "Look, Susie, at my shoes. My mother bought me new shoes from Woolworths." He say it's the latest fashion. I laugh. He's a player. You know what a player is, my baby? He's a player but he's like a girl. I know these ones. There are boys in the township like them. But God knows what He's doing and as long as he respect I don't mind. But Vera – yo yo yo – she is a bad lady. Sophie she tell me that the daughter – Petrus sister – what's her name? Something funny . . .'

'Lizelle?'

'Yes – this one – she go out every night. She have a lot of boyfriends. One day, Jack, that one is going to have a baby and then the black people will laugh. Yo yo yo – we will laugh at this Vera bitch. We will say – yes – you see, the *tokoloshe* put the baby in that girl's tummy. Jack! You laugh at me?'

'No,' I said, laughing into my sleeve.

'The *tokoloshe* know about the man's thing. He can make a man's thing big and strong when it's better that it's small and weak like my finger. And the *tokoloshe* can make man's thing small and weak when it's better that it's big and strong. You mustn't laugh at the *tokoloshe*. He will give you a small thingy.' I blushed. This was not something to laugh about. It wasn't worth taking any chances where small thingies were concerned.

6

Tannie Vera has a dismembered kudu

WHEN PETRUS FINALLY walked into the kitchen he had changed into a pair of purple shorts, a yellow T-shirt and leather sandals. He stood at the door hesitantly, his hand stroking the door frame.

'Must you forever be wearing shoes?' she asked.

His habit of always wearing shoes, even in the house, irritated her because it irritated her husband. Oom Frik would talk about how, when he was a child, he crossed the veld and scaled the koppies without shoes. A real Afrikaner boy would brush the *duwweltjies* – the small thorns – from his feet.

'Are you two going to play outside?'

'No, Mom, in my room.'

Tannie Vera sighed. 'Why can't you play outside like a normal boy? What did your father build that tree house for? He spent the whole weekend building that thing so you would spend some time outside but I don't think he's seen you play in it once. At least take off those sandals before he gets home.'

Things were difficult between Petrus and his father. His presence was a source of irritation to the man. But Petrus *was* peculiar. When I said before that he seemed a much more likely product of my odd, soft family, that's not to say that my parents wouldn't have regarded him as strange. That's not to say that my parents wouldn't have been disturbed by his odd behaviour. I used to play a game with Emmanuel called Hospital Hospital. It was a very elementary sort of game and in its own way, I suppose, odd too. Emmanuel and I would pretend to be mountain climbers or lorry drivers or aircraft pilots. We would sit on the jungle gym and I would say, 'Look, Emmanuel, I'm climbing a mountain,' and Emmanuel would say, 'Look, I'm driving a lorry,' and then I would say, 'Oh no, I'm falling off the mountain! I've fallen down the mountain and had a terrible accident. Everyone thinks I am going to die,' and Emmanuel would say, 'Oh no, the brakes aren't working – I'm going to crash, I'm crashing! Everyone thinks I am going to die,' and then we would both be admitted to hospital with terrible and life-threatening injuries and everyone would be convinced that we were going to die. And then we would lie around in hospital recuperating from our terrible injuries for hours and hours. Hospital Hospital was definitely our favourite game. Sometimes we *would* die. I would say, 'Now I'm dead,' and he would say, 'Me too,' and then we'd start all over again; 'Look, I'm driving a lorry . . .' Both Emmanuel and I loved the idea of going to hospital. Once Emmanuel climbed over a wire fence and sliced his ball sack open, but this wasn't the sort of experience he had in mind.

I liked the Hospital Hospital game so much that I introduced it to Petrus. I wanted to play it all day long.

'Look, Petrus, I'm flying an airplane,' I said.

'Is it South African Airways?'

'It doesn't matter.'

'Yes it does.'

'OK, it's Swissair.'

'Swissair is the best airline in the world.'

'I know.'

'OK, can I be an air hostess?'

'No, why don't you drive a lorry?'

'I don't want to drive a lorry.'

'OK, why don't you climb a mountain?'

'I don't like climbing'

'OK, you can be an air hostess.'

'Where is first class?'

'It doesn't matter.'

'But you have to serve the people in first class before you help the other people.'

'This is first class. Behind me.'

'I'm going to make coffee while you fly the airplane. Is it a Boeing or an Airbus?'

'It's a Boeing. Oh no! The engines have stopped working.'

'Wait – I haven't finished making coffee.'

'It's too late! We're going to crash! Oh no . . . we're craaaaaasssshiiiiinnngggg.' I lay on the ground with my tongue sticking out. 'Petrus! What are you doing?'

'I'm helping the people in first class.'

'No, Petrus, you're not. They're all dead. You're nearly dead too. Lie on the ground and wait for the ambulance.' Safely hospitalised I said, 'My legs are broken, my arms are broken. I've broken all my ribs. My neck is broken and I can't move. Everyone thinks I'm going to die. What's wrong with you?'

'They've cut off my *tottie*. Now I have to be a lady for the rest of my life.'

'Let's go and play Lego.'

It's no surprise that the boy was the recipient of some pretty severe canings – not child-abuse-severe, but sufficient to leave some nasty marks on his buttocks. I was terrified of Oom Frik too. Of course, we all thought that he hoped to beat the *moffie* right out of the boy. *Now* we know that this sort of thinking, however well intentioned, just leads to a different *kind* of *moffie*. It was not unheard of for parents to occasionally beat their son's friends but this was frowned upon. I wouldn't have put it past Oom Frik if the occasion warranted it, but generally I was (at least in the company of friends) a well-behaved child. This is the moderately felicitous outcome of crossing the English with the Afrikaners; the two races can temper the other's worst excesses. So though my family had none of the frugality of the Afrikaners, we did have their discipline. I also received the occasional hiding – once or twice even in public – though this was something my father did very rarely. I forgave my father for the hidings. They were, though I didn't know the word for it, primal. They stemmed from an irrational rage deep within. They were crimes of passion. When I told my sensitive godfather that he was 'short some hair in his head' my father could not contain the eruption of his anger. He didn't sit down like Oom Frik or the schoolteachers and make a cold-blooded decision about the degree of pain to inflict. If my father had had time to sit down and think about it I don't think he would ever have raised a finger against me. To give someone a hiding like Oom Frik did was like an execution. It would be done at an appointed time and an appointed place: after dinner, with a cane, in the study, like a murder in Cluedo. It was also, I felt, less effective, for it engendered in young Petrus an understanding of the economy of crime.

A disobedience might be weighed against the severity of the probable punishment. But if your father suddenly and unexpectedly lost all sense of control and gave you the hiding of your life, you quickly learnt how to stop driving another human being into a fit of apoplectic rage. It was an enlightening moment for a child. There came a time of course when a child outgrew this form of punishment. Mothers, we all agreed, should desist from spanking when they found themselves chasing the delinquent child around the house with a sneaker in hand. This was undignified and unhelpful. Fathers could get away with it for a little longer, until perhaps the eleventh birthday (for girls) and the twelfth birthday (for boys). Afrikaners, the English thought, always had to take things a little too far and could still be found caning their seventeen-year-old sons for smoking behind the garden shed or stealing beer out of the fridge.

Emmanuel and Thomas, being English, were never caned and nor I believe was Aaron, who was Jewish, but that might have been because he was just so big for his age. Mr Grossman used to cane Jürgen, but then he died and Mrs Grossman didn't take it up. Having said that, Afrikaans fathers also kissed their sons, *on the lips*. And not only prepubescent boys. Even when I was eighteen my father kissed me *on the lips*. And I never thought anything peculiar about this.

'I think,' Petrus said as he crawled under the bed to retrieve the book, 'they read it before they have sex.' In other countries, boys of our age may well have discovered in their parents' bedrooms or at friends' houses an erotic or pornographic picture of some kind. In other countries, boys might have found in a seedy local store a proprietor who turned a blind eye to the healthy interest of near adolescents. But to the South African censors, the darkening that was the areola was prurient and as such deemed objectionable. Men sometimes boasted of smuggling *Playboy* past the ever-vigilant customs agents, but we took these stories to be apocryphal for we had never seen a copy. This book, *The Illustrated Married Couple's Guide to Better Love Making*, illegally imported from Lesotho, exceeded to a very significant degree my expectations of what picture books might contain, particularly the chapter entitled 'Sexual Positions'. The clinical descriptions we had heard came vividly to life in a series of pencil sketches. Not only could men lie on top of women, couples could lie side by side. Women could straddle men, backwards and forwards. It was even possible to have sex as animals did – from behind! This artist, I thought, was extraordinarily well versed in the infinite possibilities of the erotic. I could not see how, without instruction, I could ever have found such variance in what was, after all, the same act.

On one page was a drawing of a man having sex with the woman from behind. The man's head was thrown back. How magnificent it was to be a strong virile man, with muscular thighs, powerful arms and a big penis. If I looked anything like this, I thought, I would walk around in a constant state of excitement, aroused by my own masculinity.

'Do you think he's putting it into her bottom?' Petrus asked.

'Don't be stupid,' I said, 'he must put it into her vagina.'

'My brother says you can see films with people having sex at Sun City.'

'Ja.'

'You can do lots of things at Sun City,' Petrus said. 'At Sun City there are ladies who dance onstage and show you their boobs. One day I want to go there. The ladies wear costumes with feathers and tiaras, like in Miss South Africa.'

Petrus took the book and paged through it.

'Have you seen this?' he asked. 'Sometimes the lady puts your *tottie* in her mouth.' He pointed to the picture; another revelation. Incredible the things this woman did! How magnificent! I traced the outline of the woman's back with my finger. I flipped to another page and touched between her legs. Again I flipped the page and touched where the man was penetrating the woman. I tried to will the illustrated pleasure to life. I wanted to imprint these pictures in my mind. The woman's hair was hanging over her face and her mouth was slightly open. Her hands were spread on the ground and her heavy breasts with large nipples were hanging forward. The man had his hands around her waist and his flat stomach was touching the back of her bottom. The muscles in his thighs were taut and a vein was visible in his neck. We were so absorbed in the book that we did not hear Letsatsi walking down the passage with the pile of folded laundry. When she opened the door, I slammed the book shut and stuffed it under a pillow. Letsatsi walked to the cupboard.

'What are you doing?' she asked.

'Nothing,' Petrus said.

Letsatsi placed the folded clothes in the cupboard. She removed a wire coat hanger and on this hung a freshly ironed school shirt, a pair of grey pants and the maroon school blazer with gold stripes. She picked a tie up from the floor and threaded it over the hanger, careful not to crease the shirt. Finally she examined the school uniform before hanging it on the knob of the cupboard door. With her back still turned she said, 'That is your mother's book.'

Petrus stared at his feet and didn't answer. Now we were co-conspirators who shared in the knowledge of Mrs Steyn's carnality: varicose veins spread wide; legs with varicose veins wrapped around the portly frame of her balding husband, the angry builder; and on the bedside table a pair of bifocals with a plaited grey cord, hanging limp over the table edge. Petrus grabbed the book and rushed out of the room. With a smile, Letsatsi repacked underpants and socks. Inside, Letsatsi and I were laughing at Tannie Vera. What did a woman with five children want with a book like this? What did a woman with chickens in the backyard and a freezer filled with a dismembered kudu want with a book like this?

I walked home from Petrus's house in a daze. Pre-adolescents were not designed for this quantity of frank and anatomically accurate information. My sexual circuits were fried. In fact, it seemed a waste. A small fraction of that information would have served me well for many months and now I had a veritable library of information to catalogue and consult; it seemed certain that something revelatory, something critical, would be misfiled and forgotten.

I never really discussed the topic of masturbation with any of my friends. I discovered it by accident while fondling my willy in the bath. Afterwards I lay in the tepid water, a little shaken. My puritan streak eventually got the better of me: it was impossible that something which felt so good, which was so easily achieved, could be without dire conse-quences, could be an act not wholly corrupting and dangerous and degenerative in some way. Was it possible to tug it right off? It was such a personal and shameful thing that I couldn't find a way to discuss the matter with Petrus. I didn't know that Petrus *had* in fact raised the matter when he said, 'Jack, do you like to *skommel*?' I didn't understand the question. I knew *skommel* meant 'to beat' so I assumed he was asking whether I liked to help with baking. I said, 'Don't be stupid. Only girls and *moffies* like to *skommel*.' But the truth was I *skommelled* constantly: in the bath, in the toilet, in the garden, at friends' houses and at night before going to bed. I *skommelled* out of habit and boredom but never mentioned it to anyone. And when I finally got my head around the mechanics of human reproduction, that there was more to masturbating than an orgasm, that at some time I could expect a thick stream of ejaculate, I became obsessed with the idea. When, I needed to know, would this miraculous thing happen? Each time I masturbated it was a temporal marker of a slow biological process that could not happen fast enough. One day I would masturbate and produce no sperm. The next day, there would be. How might my body become capable of something overnight? Was I in fact producing minute quantities that I could not detect? Would I look down to find a tiny white droplet on the tip of my dick?

I imagined some day in which my brain, having overseen the construction of whatever was necessary to produce this magnificent stuff, gave word to whoever down there was responsible for these things, to open the sluices and release the pressure of all that yearning in a glorious stream of semen. This obsession with my puberty, my own fertility, meant that my sexual fantasies were centred on myself as an adolescent, tall and strong, able to shoot jets of sperm and father a child. This narcissism did not strike me as at all odd. I was hopelessly in love with my future self.

Being neither English nor Afrikaans, being this peculiar hybrid, there was for me, aged eleven, no rite of passage into manhood. If you were Afrikaans your father might take you hunting and you'd shoot your first impala or whatever. If you were Xhosa you were dragged out into the bush and you would be circumcised, not a good practice admittedly, but still something. Being Gentile there were no bar mitzvahs and being an atheist I didn't even have a lame confirmation. So a little bit of measly jism had to stand in for an awful lot of what other cultures supplied in such abundance.

I was not alone, there were lots of colourless, characterless boys without culture like me, looking for some rite, some ceremony, some agreed-upon event to mark this passage. Now, there were some things that stood in for other more ancient and venerated ceremonies, including a ride on the Looping Star – the only roller coaster I knew of with a loop. For better or worse, my jism-less eleven-year-old self fixed on that rickety old roller coaster. As rites of passage go, it wasn't the worst choice. It really was rickety and old and, though improbable, it wasn't impossible that I could meet a nasty end while riding it. It might have marked a courage, of sorts. Unfortunately, my parents refused to take the family to the Rand Easter Show – the only opportunity that presented itself to ride the Looping Star. My parents loathed the Rand Easter Show. It was mainly full of grubby salesmen flogging washing machines, swimming pools and jacuzzis. My parents (and in particular my mother) were constitutionally opposed to jacuzzis. In this they were an oddity. Jacuzzis were not nearly so tacky in South Africa as they were in the rest of the world, and were not the sole preserve of swingers and their ilk. My mother thought there was something unhealthy about water being kept warm for so long, indefinitely even, and was also concerned about people's tendency to urinate in them.

'People pee in jacuzzis and there isn't a lot of water in them. It's not the same as peeing in swimming pools. I don't mind so much when people do that,' she said. The real reason my mother didn't like jacuzzis was that she thought they were sexy. There can be no denying that it is sexual for near-naked people to cram themselves into an oversized bathtub and it is sexual to have your genitals caressed by warm jets of water. Perhaps it was not only the pee she was worried about. Also, there was, to appease the puritan in her, a small penance to be paid for taking a swim in a pool: the unpleasant shock of first dipping into cold water. My family was not comfortable with anything that was *entirely* pleasant.

I, on the other hand, thought jacuzzis wonderful. The first time I ever saw people having sex was in a jacuzzi. Not long after Mr Grossman died of spine cancer, Mrs Grossman decided to give her son a treat so she took him (and his friends) to Warm Baths – a hot-water spring beloved of German immigrants. When I saw that the stories I had heard about German women were not apocryphal, that Mrs Grossman's pubic thatch extended to her knees almost, and that thick tufts of hair protruded from her armpits, I spent as much time away from the grieving family as an eleven-year-old thought polite, and in doing so stumbled across a couple having sex in the jacuzzi. The point being that although I wanted to go to the Rand Easter Show for the Looping Star, for me the jacuzzis were an *added* attraction, no matter how much my parents disliked them.

My parents didn't say it had anything to do with the

jacuzzis; it was not as if they made you get into them. And even if it was positively a requirement, my mother, a feisty woman, would not have been manhandled into a cesspool of piss and semen. No, my parents *said* it was the threat of bombs. The threat of bombs did not hold much water for us. Even eleven-year-olds appreciated that the ANC were rather inexpert in the construction thereof. I do not wish to cast aspersions, perhaps their Soviet teachers were to blame, but there were far more stories about some hapless do-gooder who managed to blow his hands off in an attempt to strike a blow against the evil regime, than stories about people who had successfully detonated a bomb when they were not within lethal or disfiguring distance of it. So the ANC and their struggle were also good (I mean good in addition to fighting a moral and courageous war) in that they provided my parents with a convenient ruse for denying me trips to the Rand Easter Show.

The threat of terrorism was pervasive. In all the schools I attended there was a large and expensively produced chart of bombs and landmines. The devices were rendered in three-dimensional plastic like a military pop-up book. The rationale behind this chart was unclear to us at the time. It is not, we thought, as if we are so stupid that we might mistake *that* for something innocuous. A Russian military landmine does not share an unfortunate resemblance with anything else you are likely to find in a primary school, or even a high school for that matter. Nevertheless, we duly followed instructions to check under our desks for anything suspicious, particularly anything that resembled something appearing on the chart. Even though we never really thought that the ANC would blow up classrooms, the constant reminder, that in the grand scheme of things they had to consider certain whites dispensable, was enough to make us all a little wary – and so when my parents said, 'We're not going to the Rand Easter Show because there might be bombs,' there wasn't very much an eleven-year-old boy could say. So I never did get to ride on the Looping Star and had to wait for another two and half years to be assured that I was in fact a man, as much as anyone else, as much even as Anton.

As I walked towards the swimming pool I was relieved that Percy was nowhere to be seen. I needed time to consider the sex book. The lady in the picture had much bigger boobs than Amie who sat next to me in history class. Amie was from Mauritius and had pert little breasts that I longed to touch. I believed, though I wasn't sure, that she was part Creole, which added a certain frisson to my desire. Part Creole meant she wasn't entirely white. I sat on the pool ledge and placed the heel of my foot into the outlet jet. Amie wore her dress very short and took her scrunchy out of her hair at break times so that her dark curls tumbled down and caressed her soft caramel-coloured arms. My erection pressed painfully against the inner lining of my costume but it didn't matter. It wasn't like our school Speedos. The remains of a bloated Parktown prawn cricket floated by. I picked it up by one its spiny legs and flung it on to the grass. Sammy ran over and started chewing it. The crunching sounds made me feel queasy. Amie was surly with teachers who, I was sure, envied her beauty. She spent many afternoons in Mrs Hennings's classroom but rarely did I see her emerge with puffy eyes, newly contrite. She was the type of girl of whom Mrs Hennings would have said 'vroeg ryp, vroeg vrot,' which means 'early ripe, early rotten'. Indeed, this proved to be so, for in her fifteenth year Amie blew one of the De Jesus brothers ('A filthy Leb,' Aaron had called him) behind the bike shed – an incident wittily referred to as the 'Coming of the Lord'. I did not understand the mechanics of bras. It was possible that Amie's breasts were as big as the lady's from the book; unleashed they might swell like those plastic toys you put in water. I sat on the pool step and slipped my hands into my pants. Placing my index finger on the tip of my willy, I pulled my foreskin over my second knuckle.

Everyody liked Amie, including Mr Novak who came from Czechosolvakia or Poland or one of those countries that would definitely be on Russia's side if ever we went to war. He always asked the pretty girls to stay after class for an extra lesson and though some girls were only chosen once or twice we agreed that Amie was lucky because she got chosen more than anyone else. The person who loved Amie most of all was Aaron, but unlike the rest of us, she was not won over by his generous man dick. He showed it to her once. The only person Amie liked was Chad, the boy from the orphanage. So it was that Amie and Chad took starring roles in my fantasies.

I positioned my crotch in front of the outlet jet. It felt good.

'Amie,' I said, testing the words, 'you have such beautiful hair.'

'Thanks, Chad,' I said. 'You have such strong arms.'

'I'm training to be an acrobat. Vladimir says I have an acrobat's muscles. You know, Amie, you have a lovely vagina for a coloured.'

'Chad,' I said, 'you have the hairiest *tottie* on the cricket A team.'

'Thanks, Amie. Can I put my *tottie* in your mouth?'

'Yes, Chad. It feels so good when you put your *tottie* in

my mouth.' I slipped down my pants and held my willy in the centre of the powerful current.

'Oh, Amie!' I said.

'Oh, Chad!' I said.

'Oh, Amie!' I said.

'Oh, Chad!' I said.

'Oh, Amie, I'm going to sperm.'

Waves of pleasure rippled from my groin and I had to hold on to the pool ledge to steady myself. It would have been wonderful, were it not for the fact that from across the garden I heard someone giggling. Percy was sitting on the stoep, sipping a can of Coke. I was paralysed with shame.

'Jesus,' I said for the first time in life. 'Jesus Christ.'

'Oh, Chad!' he said in girlish mimicry.

'Go away!' I said, nearly in tears, but Percy did not move and started laughing out loud. 'I hate you!' I screamed as I pulled up my pants. Susie came running out of the house.

'What's going on?' she said.

'Nothing.' I grabbed my towel and raced inside the house. Susie followed.

'Jack! What happened? Did Percy do something? Did he hit you, my boy?'

'Leave me alone!'

'I will hit him for you, my boy. I will hit him. Tell me, Jack – what Percy do?'

'Nothing, Susie – he didn't do anything – just leave me alone! Go and do your ironing.'

'Jack – you mustn't talk to me like this. I will tell your daddy you talk to me like this. I am going to talk to Percy – I am going to ask him about this thing.'

'No!' I shouted. 'Don't talk to Percy – whatever he says is lies.'

'Jack?'

'He's a liar. He's a big liar. And you should tell him to mind his own business. You should tell him it's very rude to spy on people. He has no manners.'

'Jack? Why you say this thing?'

'Because I hate him.' I went to my bedroom and slammed the door behind me. I could feel the shame and the rage in my chest and in my stomach. I picked up a He-Man figurine and hurled it against the cupboard. How dare he? How dare he spy on me? How dare he laugh at me? He didn't even have a standard seven. He was always tormenting me. This was *my* house. He was a *guest*. He probably thought I was a *moffie* like Petrus. He would never understand that I just thought Chad was handsome and there wasn't anything sexy about it. I might look at Chad's willy in the changing rooms but that didn't mean anything. I liked to look at everyone's willies. It was impossible that I was a *moffie* for many reasons, but most of all because, unlike Petrus, I *did* walk barefoot almost everywhere. The only time I wore shoes was when I *had* to wear shoes, when I was *told* to wear shoes, and in the Afrikaans school in summer when we were allowed to come to school barefoot, I *did* and Petrus *didn't*. I even went to the mall barefoot, and when I went on the escalators, people would sometimes point at the sign that said '*Geen Kaal Voete / No Bare Feet*' and I would say, 'Don't worry, Tannie, I never get my toes caught in the escalator,' even though there *was* a story about a kid in *You Magazine*, who got caught in an escalator and *died*. This showed that I was tough. I would swim out to the shark nets when we went on holiday to Durban and Petrus would never do that because he was too busy pretending to be a mermaid, which I would never do. And when Petrus and I picked up jacaranda flowers and sucked the nectar out the end, because it tasted a bit like honey, like flower-flavoured honey, I didn't scream like a girl when instead of nectar I got a mouthful of little bugs instead. And I didn't like girlie things at all, and when we played Hospital Hospital, I never, ever pretended anything had happened to my *tottie*, I would never say, 'They've cut off my *tottie* and now I have to be a girl.' Because I *loved totties*. So there was no way that I was a *moffie*. I picked up another He-Man doll and hurled it at the cupboard again. Its head snapped off and I was immediately sorry. A whole month's pocket money wasted.

'Jack!' Susie shouted from downstairs. 'Are you throwing things?'

'No, Susie.'

'Don't throw things!'

I sat on my bed. Now Percy knew things about me that nobody else did. Not my mother or father or my sisters or Petrus. He knew I thought about things that were dirty and perverted and that I thought about girls, but also that I thought about boys. I was sorry about what I'd said at the OK Bazaar, but it didn't give him the right to spy. A civilised person, I thought, would avert their eyes. A civilised person would have walked back inside. A civilised person would not intrude upon your most private moments and gawp and stare and laugh. Sometimes one had to wonder whether those angry Boers didn't have a point. One had to wonder whether Petrus and Tannie Vera and Oom Frik and my aunts and uncles didn't have a very good point. Percy was now my enemy. And though it was terrible in ways I could not quite comprehend, I was white and Percy was black which made me powerful in ways that should have given Percy second thoughts before laughing at me in the swimming pool.

7

Corpse-sized refrigerators

I CAME IN and leant carefully on the bed. Ouma's bones broke easily, or at least that is what my mother said: 'Be careful or you will break Ouma's bones!' I kissed her on the cheek.

'Hello, child,' she said.

Because Ouma was dying, everyone lied to her.

'I still do piano lessons – grade 6, Ouma. And I got my report card. All A's, Ouma.'

'That's good, my child,' she said. 'You have your father's brains.' I glanced at my mother. 'The Dominee visited me yesterday.'

My parents called the minister at the local Dutch Reformed Church 'the poisonous dwarf'. His manner was obsequious and his church was rich. But because Ouma would soon be dead we had to keep on his good side so that he would help with the funeral.

'He's written about me in the newsletter.'

She reached for the bedside cabinet. I opened the drawer and removed the newsletter she had shown us last week.

'Is it this one, Ouma?' I asked.

'Let me see.' She held it to her nose, squinting at the letters. 'Yes, this is the one. It was a very nice thing for him to write this.'

At the last party for Ouma, her seventy-fifth birthday, I discovered that the mad psychiatrist had moved into the playroom at the back of his garden. He declined to come up and visit the guests, preferring to sit outside in his underpants, record player blaring, tanning his big hairy face in the summer sun. I asked whether my uncle and aunt were now divorced, to which my mother replied, 'Not really, but as good as.' This sounded a bit like Susie and Lebo. Perhaps they were 'estranged' even though they still lived on the same property.

Now that there were no more parties for Ouma, the families were careful to time their visits to the old-age home to avoid one another. The next time we would have to talk would be at Ouma's funeral, the arrangement of which occupied her a great deal. She had seen a television advert in which the presenter implied that one's death was likely to be a terrible burden to friends and family. I do not think she wanted the pervading mood of her departure to be one of inconvenience. So the adults connived in a fantasy in which she had prudently set aside funds for the purpose of her 'disposal', as my father snapped one day, when he tired of discussing the matter.

Watching my grandmother and my father I learnt something about how the relationship between a son and his mother developed over time. At some point, I concluded, there was a shift so that it resembled more the relationship between a husband and a wife. As the mother aged so too the son grew into his father, and recognising the familiar patterns, the mood swings, the sudden temper, the behaviours of old emerged and the mother was walking on eggshells again, as she had twenty years before when her bad-tempered husband returned from work.

Ouma sat in bed, wide-eyed. She knew what the procession of visitors meant. She no longer saw the doctor, and every few hours the nurse popped her head round the door to see if she was still alive. Ouma could not complain. She could not tell people she was afraid. She had, since any of us could remember, been waiting for her bony shoulder blades to sprout wings; she pined openly for Jesus and Daphne; she spoke about the joyous release of death. But in her eyes I could see a child who had awoken from a nightmare and is too scared to fall back asleep. We willed Ouma to death – but she rallied.

'Have a little rest. You look tired,' we said.

'Did I tell you about Daphne?' she asked.

'Tell us tomorrow,' we said.

The nurse put her head round the door. 'Is everything OK?'

'Everything is OK, thank you.'

What could we say? No, something truly catastrophic is going to happen, but it is nothing also. We are hurtling along at breakneck speed and someone is about to fall off and be left alone in the dark, but she's hanging on with her fingernails and we want to prise them loose because we're tired and we want to go home, we want this to be over, but everything is OK.

In the background we could hear the faint hum of the ward. Nurses and maids were talking quietly in the corridors. Occasionally the phone would ring. These were the gentle and innocuous rhythms of an operation, which tended, fed, cleaned, soothed and maintained two dozen bodies awaiting dispatch. The system was brisk but not hurried, subdued but not sad, sterile but not clinical. Like midwives, the staff seemed to be possessed of a matriarchal wisdom, the sturdy and unattractive women of a tribe born to live here, who took pride in their detachment and cultivated a comforting cynicism which grew from watching people fade out of existence with less drama than their arrival. What was the significance of witnessing a person's last moment anyway?

I was not actually there when Ouma died, but I imagined that it happened in a moment of inattentiveness, when my aunts or my father looked away, perhaps staring out at the gardens, when she suddenly, miraculously, died and they thought: like a watched pot. The faint hum continued and in the kitchens the maids lifted the giant urns on to the trolleys for the morning breakfast round. I imagined these things because one did not ask. That would be rude.

A few years later my uncle the physicist said, 'Thank God my mother is dead. Imagine if she had to see Gaddafi and Castro on South African soil?'

When my mother called me into the kitchen to tell me that Ouma died, she said, 'Ouma died this morning.'

As I suspected, it was embarrassing. What was I to say to my mother? I'm sorry?

'I'm sorry,' I said.

This was my first death. I felt guilty for not feeling sad. When, a year earlier, I saw a man run over on the highway, I cried in the car. I cried when a Zulu warrior was stabbed in a television series. I cried when I broke my favourite toy. I considered myself peculiarly susceptible to grief, but now I could find no trace of it. I could only think how curious it was that I knew someone who had died. This should enrich me. In time more and more people would die, and one day, when I was as old as Ouma, I would know more dead people than living people. I wondered if my grand-mother was in heaven and if so whether she could read my thoughts. What would she make of this? Would she be disappointed by my indifference? Dead, was she blessed with divine understanding? In my mind, dead people were one with God, a great intermingling of the supernatural; Our Lord Ouma. She would be terrible and powerful like God. Of course, she might just be dead. This was what my father believed. Dead in the same way that you were dead before you were born for millions and millions of years, stretching back into infinity. And of this my father said, 'It didn't worry you then, did it?' Intellectually my father was a man of small mercy. Jesus, that dead man on a stick, was an appropriate symbol for those people who had been broken by life.

In my short life I had had two experiences of the divine. When I was six, my parents sent me to Sunday school. They thought this the most prudent course of action for my social development, it being essential to have a passing familiarity with Noah and his ark, Abraham and his people, Jesus and his resurrection. And to the question that would undoubtedly be posed, 'To which church do you belong?' I could safely answer, 'The Dutch Reformed Church, Miss.'

The Sunday-school lessons were inoffensive. The teachers never said a word against the Jews or the Catholics. At the end of the year a star would be added to each child's diploma. Children who collected seven stars graduated from Sunday school and could attend church with their parents. Once a month a special children's service was held so that we might receive some religious instruction from the minister. Bripsies, burps and giggles would only happen in God's peripheral vision, the primary purpose of the service being not devotional but instructional. The finer points of etiquette needed to be learnt. This also allowed the church to introduce, at an early age, the custom of tithing. The claim that God made upon the pocket money of a six-year-old developed into a habit hard to break oneself of. On one occasion, the minister forgot to send round the collection plate and I realised that I had in my possession money, the existence of which was known only to me and Jesus. Deities have precarious tenure in the minds of six-year-olds, particularly on warm afternoons with all their promise of illicit pleasures such as chips and ice cream. I spent all of God's money and that evening He came crashing rudely into my mind, like a tidal wave, a creature of such awesome enormity that it breached with ease the faculties of a child. I lay rigid, waiting for divine wrath. If God spoke, which I knew from my lessons He was apt to do, I would die of fright. All night I tossed and turned, until I saw the first rays of the sunrise and slept for an hour in the comfort that God had been banished for the day. (Incidentally, and Sunday-school lessons notwithstanding, I still had a great deal to learn about the finer points of Afrikaners and religion. Within my first week of primary school I was accused of blasphemy, when, in my drawing of Palm Sunday, I included a picture of Christ triumphantly astride a donkey. We were only permitted to represent Jesus as a diffuse golden glow using Faber-Castell Sunlight Yellow pencil shavings. In my attempts to rectify the picture, Jesus soon looked like a black man who had urinated on Winnie-the-Pooh's melancholy friend.)

My second experience of the divine occurred when, in a Sunday-school lesson about the young Jesus, the most blasphemous thought of my life took hold: could I too be the son of God? It was impossible to unthink the thought and all my attempts to obliterate it from my memory fuelled the idea until it became more and more insistent, like a voice trying to reason with the unwilling recipient of a message, trying to tell me what I did not wish to hear. An astute person might well have regarded this moment as an insight into the genesis of psychopathology. I fell to my knees and begged God for forgiveness.

But by the time Ouma died I had weighed things up and decided I wasn't too fond of God. An easy thing, one might think, for the child of atheists to say, but *I* believed, to a degree. I might have been precocious but I wasn't particularly smart. It wasn't the problem of evil that militated against God's existence – that didn't seem to bother me in the least; it was his Afrikaans-ness. More and more he seemed like Oom Frik or my uncle on a supernatural scale. That little epithet – I am the light – reminded me of the prison cells on Death Row. God simply had no respect for anyone's privacy. Decent human beings knew when to avert their eyes. Well-behaved human beings pretended they hadn't caught you picking your nose or jacking off. But the funeral was an opportunity for God to redeem Himself. We would gather to entrust Ouma's soul to His care. And in the same way that prize-giving was different from run-of-the-mill assemblies, I was hoping for something a little special.

My family shared a distaste for small talk, for the obsequious manner, the unctuous patter of men who sold for a living. We disliked haggling and were resigned to paying simply what was asked. We would not permit pleasantries or allow ourselves to be seduced by the enjoyment of making a purchase. For us, life was a series of necessary exchanges, some more distasteful than others, few as distasteful as this:

> Superior handcrafted, solid wood casket. Triple layer, split hinged lid with glass viewing panel. Featuring elegant mouldings and fluted corner columns. Brass-effect extended bar handles and brass-effect nameplate. Luxury satin interior.

The undertaker leant across the desk, flipped through the brochure and pointed to the bottom right-hand corner.

> Basic coffin: pine with chrome handles.

'That'll do,' we said.

The body was in the morgue being embalmed. We queried this. Was it not wasteful to embalm a body that would be cremated the next day?

'Ag – that's the way it is,' the matron replied. 'Most people go straight to the mortuary to be embalmed. Hygiene rules are very strict and it happens before most families even know about it. The Jews have to be very careful. Quite often you will find out that a Jewish person has been embalmed by mistake – but usually they don't mind so much anyway. Ag, you know, with everything else that's going on it's the least of their worries. I expect it's the same with the Muslims; though obviously we don't have any Muslim residents here. I am surprised your mother wants to be cremated, it's not the way of our Church.' The Afrikaners believed that God's powers did not stretch to reconstituting cremated bodies upon Christ's return and so preferred to buy family plots in which you heaped up your dead, piled them up as evidence of your suffering; *oupa* and *ouma*, *ma* and *pa*, *boeta* and *sussie,* in a grotesque double bed. The Second Coming notwithstanding, was cremation not more in keeping with our morbid ethos? Burnt into nothingness; make no fuss, let not a trace of me remain. Do what is small and quiet and understated. Grind me back into the earth.

Of course there were still some Afrikaners who, even in the cities, insisted on doing things the old-fashioned way. In a gaudy casket the body would make its way back to the family home. Then the woman would cook and bake and relatives from far and wide would drop in to take a look and eat some milk tart. This was what real Afrikaners did. But the new Afrikaners could no longer stomach the idea of a dead body in the house. In the eyes of my family these Afrikaners were mad, feral, backward. Why live in cities equipped with corpse-sized refrigerators and corpse-sized incinerators? I liked the idea of bringing the body home. I could go to school and talk about my dead granny in the lounge. 'We kept her in the lounge,' I would say to my English friends, 'because that is the Afrikaner way. We kept her in the lounge until we buried her.'

I could not visit any of my friends that day because I had to wait until my father came home so that I could say 'I'm sorry' to him too. It would be wrong for me to come back from a friend's house, breathless, flushed, excited, and find my father sitting at the dining-room table. I was not sure whether my father was in mourning. I fetched my costume and made my way down to the pool but Percy was sitting on the stoep reading a newspaper so I went and sat in the TV room. Rachel came in and sat beside me.

'Because Ouma is dead are they going to bury her?' she asked.

'No, she's going to be cremated,' I said.

'What's cremated?'

'They put you in a fire and burn you up.'

'In a fire?' she said, tearing up.

'It doesn't matter. She's dead, she can't feel anything.'

'I don't want them to put Ouma in a fire!'

'Don't worry about it, Rachel –'

'Jack, please don't let them put Ouma in a fire!'

'OK, OK. Don't worry – they won't put Ouma in the fire. Jeez – you can be such a baby sometimes.'

'Where are they going to put Ouma then?'

'In the garden.'

'In our garden?'

'Yes.'

'Where in our garden?'

'Next to the swimming pool.'

'Really?'

'Yes.'

'I thought Ouma was going to heaven.'

'She *is* in heaven.'

'But I thought we're going to put her in the garden.'

'She stays in heaven during the day and then at night she sleeps in the garden.'

'Oh. Why did Ouma die?'

'Because she was very old.'

'What's very old?'

'As old as Mom and Dad put together.'

'That's really old. Is Ouma in heaven now?

'Yes.'

'What's she doing in heaven?'

'I don't know, Rachel, I've never been there.'

'Do you think she's in her bed watching TV?'

'Maybe.'

'Do they have TV in heaven?'

'I think so.'

'Do they have *Pumpkin Patch* in heaven? *Pumpkin Patch* is my favourite programme.'

'I know, Rachel.'

'Do they have Hi-Ho-Cherry-O in heaven?'

'No – they definitely don't have Hi-Ho-Cherry-O in heaven.'

'Oh,' she said, 'poor Ouma.'

When Susie heard she said, 'I can't believe she's dead!' which I thought a silly thing to say really because it wasn't so unbelievable at all. Susie reacted with surprise when anyone died, as if this was the only polite response, as if she thought them capable of a great many things but not the effrontery of dying.

Rachel and I were sitting in the backyard with Susie. She'd laid out an old blanket on which she placed all the forks, knives and spoons. Beside her stood a bottle of Silvo. The smell made your eyes sting and your nose burn. It was delicious.

'She was a nice lady. A real Boer! A real Afrikaner! When my granny die, I cry for a long time. My granny was like my mother. She raised me. Not my mother. My mother I love her, but my granny was like my true mother, my real mother. One day when I die, Jack, you must come to my funeral.'

'I'll come to you funeral,' Rachel said.

'Ah, this one is too sweet. Thank you, Rachie.'

'My name's not Rachie, my name is Rachel.'

'Ha ha ha – this one – she thinks she is so big. Hey, Jack?'

'Can I do one, Susie?' Rachel asked.

'Yes – do this spoon. You must make it shiny like Mama Susie, neh? See this one? I want it to look like this one.'

'OK.'

'Here, use this cloth. Jack, you and your sister must make me a nice tombstone. You, when you are big, you will be rich like your daddy and I know you love me. So you must make me a nice grave and a nice tombstone. You know, Jack, I have no money to pay for my granny's tombstone. It's more than one thousand. It's too much. But it's bad. What the people say about me? They come, they say, Susie doesn't give her grandmother a proper burial. She doesn't love her granny. The ancestors will be mad for me.' She still made guilty visits to the witch doctor to keep in abeyance the other spectral sphere, for she was undecided about the outcome of a showdown between Christ and her formidable grandmother.

'The witch doctor he say my ancestors are mad! He say they have a very big temper. He say I must pay him one hundred – we slaughter the goat." I say to him, "*One hundred* – are you crazy?!" Jack, I laugh when he tell me this thing. I tell him, "I will buy a cheap goat." He says to me, "Susie, no." He says to me, "Susie, you must get the special goat from me." But I say to him he must . . .' She glanced at Rachel and then whispered to me, 'I say he must fok off! Yes, I say to him – he must fok off.'

'Did you say a swear, Susie?' Rachel asked. 'Mom says if I say swears she will wash my mouth out with soap.'

'Yes, Rachie – your mom is right. Jack, I say to him, I already give him fifty rand. I say to him, "What my granny want with a goat? She's dead, I am alive." Yes. I tell him. But I *must* buy the tombstone. I must. One thousand is a lot of money. Me, I am poor. I say to Lebo, he must stop being so stingy. He must pay for my granny's tombstone. He get so angry, Jack! He say, "Why must I pay? Your family must pay! Your mother must pay!" But this is not right.

It doesn't matter if it's *your* family or *my* family. When someone die, you give them a nice burial and you give them a nice tombstone. I say to him when he die, I am going to throw him on the rubbish dump!' She laughed as she said this. 'Yes! I put that *stutla* man and his ZCC robes in a big plastic bag and I throw him! Ha ha!'

'Jack says we're going to put Ouma in the garden,' Rachel said.

'Jack! What you tell your little sister?'

'She's lying. I never said that.'

'He did, Susie. He said we're going to put Ouma next to the swimming pool.'

Susie laughed. 'Rachie – you mustn't listen to your brother. This one, he is a liar. He is a big liar. You think your mommy and daddy bury your granny in the garden? For what, Rachie?'

'My name's not Rachie, my name is Rachel.'

'Ai – this one. What she think, Jack? She think she is a woman.'

'I'm a lady,' Rachel said and Susie burst out laughing again.

'Jack, your little sister. She's so sweet this one. Rachie – I know you are sad about your granny. But you mustn't worry. Your mommy and daddy make a nice funeral and then your granny go to heaven. You know how the black people make funerals, Rachel?' She shook her head. 'You must get the ox and two sheep and some chickens and you must slaughter them.'

'What's slaughter?'

'You kill them, my baby,' Susie said. 'It cost a lot of money. A sheep is two hundred. The ox is maybe one thousand. Many people come to the funeral. And you must buy me a nice coffin. Jack – you mustn't leave me like the rubbish.

But you – you are a good boy – you are my son – I know, in my heart, I don't have to worry. And Rachel too. When I am old, you will take care of me. Both. You will say – ag, shame, Susie, she is old, we must take care of her. When I retire in Kabalazani, you must visit me before I die. Then you will see the nice house I make there. And I will say to the people, "This is Jack. He is my son. This is Rachel. She is my daughter. I raise these ones from the time they was this high. I raise them from the time they was a baby." Rachie – let me see that spoon.'

'Here, Susie.'

'Yes – this is good. You make it nice. One day, when I am old, are you going to come and clean my house for me?'

'Yes, Susie.'

'That's good. And Jack, you think Jack will do it? I don't think – your brother is too lazy!' Rachel laughed. 'What you think, Rachel? I think your brother is going be very *stutla* one day because he is so lazy!'

'And he's a liar, Susie.'

'Yes – he's a liar. Jack – I can't believe you tell your little sister this thing. What the people think? Yo yo yo – you make big stories.'

For black people, the matter of death and funerals was different. A big, black, shiny coffin with silver trim made life worth living; a big, black, shiny coffin with silver trim meant that you had lived and died but had made some money along the way. When you were eighteen and came to work as a maid, you joined a funeral fund and every month you gave thirty rand, comfortable in the knowledge that, on the day of your death, you would be going in style, held aloft, dead and serene in your big, black, shiny coffin with silver trim. Of course, black people did not really believe in death anyway. When you died you would be an ancestor. And ancestors were powerful indeed. From beyond the grave you would watch your family and if they displeased you there were any manner of terrible things you could ensure might befall them: a grisly accident in a mine, a hateful employer like Tannie Vera, unruly children, theft, impotence, disease. But if they pleased you, you had the power to intercede, to bring them wealth, and children, and good erections. It was the wrath of the ancestors that made undertakers rich. For if your granny had not been sensible, if she had not made provisions for a nice tombstone, then it might be prudent to make a parting gift, especially to one who, in the flesh, beat young Michael so ruthlessly all those years ago, and save yourself the horror of her supernatural temper.

My sister came home for the funeral. Although we were all excited to see Lisa, we were scared also because Lisa could be ferocious. My sister was like a fundamentalist but without the religious bits; she burnt bright with her own sense of righteousness and so anyone who crossed her was not only dim and foolish but probably a moral degenerate as well. So sometimes it could be a little exhausting; you had to keep your guard up at all times; you had to watch what you said and you had to watch what she said and you always had to be alert to situations that might provoke my sister.

Three years previously, when we were walking along a beach in the Eastern Cape, the family stopped to watch a man reeling in what looked like a large fish.

'Disgusting,' my sister said.

'Don't be silly,' my mother said, 'he's only fishing.' Eventually the man pulled a small shark on to the shore.

He removed the hook from its mouth and started re-baiting it. Before my parents could stop her, my sister walked over and said, 'Excuse me.'

'What?' the man said.

'Are you planning to eat that shark?'

'Do I look like a Chink?' the man said. My sister, I thought, is very brave. This man was big, with smudged blue tattoos all over his arms. Everyone knew tattoos weren't very nice. Everyone knew you should be very careful of picking a fight with someone who had tattoos. I could also make out a pink scar that ran from his ear to his collarbone. Of course it wasn't nice to kill a shark for no good reason – but it wasn't really any of my sister's business. Lisa bent down to pick it up by its tail.

'Girlie – what do you think you're doing?'

'I'm putting it back. There's no reason to kill this shark.'

'Listen here, girlie – that's my shark.'

We were still a few yards away and my mother, with a note of panic in her voice, said sharply, 'Willem.'

'Yes,' he said and walked up to my sister and the tattooed man. By now my sister was holding the shark by the tail and the man was holding the shark by the head, careful to avoid its jaws.

'Lisa,' my father said, 'it looks like you're trying to steal this gentleman's shark.'

'He doesn't want it,' she said.

'Well, I think he does.'

'He's just going to leave it to die.'

'Tell your girl to leave my bloody shark alone! Who the hell does she think she is? Did she catch this shark? It's my fucking shark!'

'Lisa – just drop the shark for a moment – please!'

'Fine!' she shouted and let go of its tail.

'I think what my daughter is trying to say,' my father said as diplomatically as he could manage, 'is that if you're not going to eat the shark – which I don't believe you are – then it does seem a shame to let it die. We would be more than happy to put it back for you.'

'Jissus!' the man said, pulling off one of his gloves and throwing it on to the beach. 'I don't care what you think. Has that shark got your name on it? Has that shark got your fucking name on it?'

'There's no need to get like that,' my father said.

'I didn't think so. So it's not your property. I caught the shark. It belongs to me. I can do with it what I like. Now, will you two fuck off?'

'Lisa, there's no reasoning with this man. Come, let's go.' And as they turned away, my sister said, almost imperceptibly, but just loud enough, the magical syllable that can turn any situation nuclear: cunt. Lisa couldn't have been much older than fifteen at the time but there was certainly something amazing and heroic in this young girl deploying that word, of all words, *that word,* against this brute of a man in defence of this half-dead shark that would, in other circumstances, have taken her hand off. It made me realise that my sister was wonderful but also frightening, that she had a mouth like a steel trap which was not only dangerous, but could instantly ensnare you in the kind of mess most people spend their lives diligently avoiding.

'What?' the man bellowed.

'Lisa!' my father shouted.

'Cunt!' my sister screamed.

'Come here, you bitch!' the man said as he lunged for my sister. My father held him off and told my sister to run.

'Mom!' I shouted. 'Stop them.'

My mother, in the most authoritative voice she could

muster, demanded that the man leave her husband alone. A small crowd gathered to watch the scuffle and it had the effect of dissipating the energy. It was silly for two grown men to fight on the beach. It was soon over. My father had a cut to his left eyebrow and the man had a small cut to his top lip. The crowd was not on our side. I could hear mutters. 'That girl has a filthy mouth.' We walked back to the hotel. At first no one spoke until at last my sister, upset by the thin trickle of blood that had dried on my father's face, said, 'I'm sorry, Daddy. I didn't mean for you to get hurt.'

'It's all right,' my father said, 'but you can't go round doing whatever you like. I'm not always going to be there.'

'But he was wrong, Daddy. It was wrong to kill that shark.'

'Yes, it was wrong. But it's his shark. He has every right to do with it what he wants.'

'Who says it's his shark? It's immoral!' she said getting flustered.

'Yes, it is. And you tried. You did your best. But there are a lot of people in this world and they all have different ideas about what's moral and what's immoral. You must do what you think is right – but it doesn't help anyone if you get yourself hurt, or worse. If that man had punched you, you still wouldn't have saved the shark. And Lisa . . .'

'Yes?'

'I never want to hear you say that word again – do I make myself clear?'

'Yes.'

I said, 'Lisa, you're very strident,' and because my father cuffed me round the back of my head, I knew that I must have used the word correctly. Of course, this was only the beginning. She never stopped saying cunt and she never stopped saying what was on her mind and she never stopped getting into fights. In all that time she was lucky, because she only got hit once and I think that was also just after she called someone else a cunt. My sister loved that word almost as much as my father did. But because this was a funeral and everyone was sombre, and the house was reasonably quiet, my sister was quiet too, and wasn't too difficult.

Matron packed Ouma's few remaining belongings into an old OK Bazaar box. It was made from stiff brown cardboard with the company's red logo printed on all four sides: OK with a large red tick. It was a strange name for a store: less than satisfactory, sufficient, the promise never to overwhelm, the promise to make do in a disappointing but functional way. But when you pack a dead person's belongings in such a box, then I think the other sense of the word must have more resonance, the small solace that must always be eked out of tragedy, the half-promise that everything will be all right.

She folded the brown and black slacks, the yellow blouse, the white blouse, the green blouse and the neatly tailored jackets which Ouma had not worn for the last five years. She folded her two nighties and her dressing gown and placed the slippers on top. In the bedside cabinet was a small pile of books written by my uncle the physicist. To have a son who wrote books was something to be proud of. The Afrikaner nation was maturing. It was mastering physics and producing its own textbooks. They had rewritten man's understanding of the world, in their own young language, making new words from bits and pieces, like molecules, until they too could build the bomb in Afrikaans, which they did.

Matron must have struggled when it came to the wig. Normally, residents would be buried or cremated with their wigs. But Ouma had not worn hers for many years and the body was gone. But to put the wig in the box with her belongings! To open the box and see the top of a dead person's head among her things? That was awful. But one could not throw a wig away. Like fillings and titanium hips, the melted lumps that remained in the furnace, did the wig not also deserve burial in consecrated ground? Was the wig not more to her than her fillings or her hip? And what would the children do with this wig? Would we run around the house chasing each other with it? Or pick it up and pretend it was a small dog, making it bark and snarl, to the amusement of our friends? In the end she packed the wig in the box with the other items. And with that, Sunnyvale Retirement Home closed the account of Maria Magdalena Viljee. The box was stored in my aunt's attic for two years and lost during her last move. After that, nothing remained of Ouma.

8

The gathering of the Boers

IT STRUCK ME, in relation to the people I knew, Jürgen, my father, Susie, Percy, my cousin, even Petrus to some extent, that I had a mercifully short list of traumatic events in my life. The shortness of the list contributed to my anxiety. It was one of the reasons why I could not escape the fear that the universe was withholding the mother lode of pain and agony, and I was certain that it would be unleashed on me at some point. Every carefree year was another black mark against my name and then – sweet Jesus – it was going to rain and thunder and sleet and snow its suffering upon me. That's why the mental list of things that *had* happened to me was so important. Most of the items on my list were horrible things I had seen happen to *other* people, which, given the paucity of trauma, still qualified. The man on the highway occupied the number-one spot. Occasionally I reflected on these events and concluded that a re-ranking was called for. It was a difficult process. I had to factor in both the emotional trauma as well as how the rankings might reflect upon my character, the hypothetical test being some situation in which some person could extract by some means this mental list.

The 'public list' served as a blueprint for my moral development, which would only be fully realised when there was absolute and genuine congruence between the private list of pains and hurts and that list which I would happily submit to external scrutiny. The loss of a favourite toy had to be suitably distant from the sight of a dead pedestrian.

The items on the list were, to my credit, largely concerned with death, whether actual (including news footage) or fictional (the death of my favourite television character). So the items on my list also included the *re-enactment* of horrible things that had happened to other people. I was easily disturbed by television; it did not, however, stop me from watching. Adding things to my list was both a source of pride – a fully formed person was one who had 'been through a lot, seen many things'. Every item on the list was a small subtraction from the excruciating suffering I believed I was destined for. My grandfather tried to chop my father up with an axe and then his mother became a matron, Jürgen's father died of cancer, my cousin's parents were getting divorced, Nicola's parents were alcoholics, children suffocated in mine dumps, Susie was black and poor with an angry son and couldn't even afford a tombstone for her granny, Petrus was a *moffie* and it made his father so angry that he beat him even though there wasn't much Petrus could do about it, Daphne contracted tetanus when she was twelve and *died* even though she gave her money to the blind, and handsome brothers lost their limbs. Something awful always happened to everyone eventually. A vivid documentary about a terminally ill woman haunted me for a long time. I pondered the eventual death of my parents but was more concerned with my own demise. I lay in bed and repeated to myself: 'One day, you will die.' With each repetition I became more anxious, until my body went cold and my stomach turned and I quivered before the fear passed.

At the end of the documentary the condemned woman listed all the symptoms ignored. I took my mother aside. I did not wish to alarm her but I was dying.

'I don't think you have ovarian cancer,' she said.

My moral development was incomplete. By rights my grandmother's death should have held the number one spot and yet her ranking at the time, fourteen, above the loss of a die-cast Mercedz Benz but below the death of Darth Vader, was a compromise born out of duty and guilt.

Ouma's funeral service was held in the retirement home. It was not, as some Afrikaners would say, 'a grand affair'. The small group of family members gathered, shook hands, exchanged pleasantries. The poisonous dwarf walked around the room talking to various family members. I felt the meaty hand of my uncle the professor on my shoulder. 'Hello, little bull.' I smiled and responded to my uncle's questions in the craven way that was expected of children – Yes, Uncle; No, Uncle; I am working hard at school, Uncle. Though I was turning English, I could still talk rings around the word 'you' as well as any Afrikaner boy. (The word 'you' was considered the height of rudeness.) This was something my English-speaking friends were not very good at. They simply were not skilled in the complex verbal gymnastics required: 'Would Uncle be so kind as to let me use one of Uncle's towels so that I may swim in Uncle's pool?' It was not uncommon for adults to refer to themselves in this way too: 'Mommy would like Mommy's children to eat all the delicious food which Mommy prepared for them.' (South Africa was responsible for many crimes and not only those against humanity.)

The professor smiled and nodded as I spoke, but the man disliked me. I was struggling to get my mouth around the Afrikaans vowels. My tongue was made lazy by English. I quivered before this mountain of a man, stuffed with the physics and God and politics that were the making of his fearsome reputation in Pretoria. When I ran out of things to say, he flashed his sharp titanium teeth and said, 'Already you talk like an Englishman,' and turned away to speak to the rest of the family he loathed.

My cousin Lourens, the former leader of The Gang, skulked in the corner. I was relieved to see that he was also dressed in school uniform. I looked at him and thought about the times when my mother would drop me off at his house on a Saturday morning, and we would work on the construction of our gang headquarters. I could hardly believe that it was *this* sullen boy who had blackmailed the gardener only three years ago.

Kagiso and his common-law wife (who was also the maid) lived a rural existence in the middle of this white suburb, for my aunt let them keep chickens, and for short periods even a goat, in the large backyard, which was overgrown and hidden from view. We liked to watch him slaughter chickens, a task at which we thought him inexpert for a black. Kagiso did not wring the chicken's neck. Instead, he cut off its head with a rusty pocketknife. It was a gruesome business and it was not uncommon for the fatally wounded chicken to escape, bleeding and screaming as it flapped around the backyard. Kagiso was one of those blacks who preferred to speak Afrikaans and so he yelled, '*Haaai! Kom hierso! Fokken chicken!*' as he chased after the animal. Lourens squealed with delight – what wonders there were for this strange child in his backyard in the middle of the city. Where else in the world could he laugh at this muscled, gleaming, bloodied black man cursing a half-dead chicken that flapped around the garden with its head hanging off? His wife made a fire in front of the cottage. This was of more interest to young Lourens than watching the gardener pluck the chicken. With his hands behind his back he gently rocked against the wall of the cottage and stared at the fire. The poor woman, who could see in his eyes what I could see in his eyes, said, 'Please, master, leave the fire. It will burn you.'

She turned her back and Lourens stole a log to make his own fire. Soon the lawn was ablaze. The gardener and his wife started shouting. He ran to fetch the hose and she ran to fetch a bucket. Lourens and I stood and watched. He pointed out patches of burning grass to the maid – 'There! There!' – who stamped on them with her battered and now blackened *tekkies*. The gardener was very angry. His black skin shone with sweat and the veins in his neck throbbed. He breathed deeply as he walked towards Lourens, and because I could see trouble brewing, because I could see murder in his eyes, I ran to the maid and stood behind her, holding on to her skirt. Kagiso then did something I had never seen happen before. He struck my cousin across the face. Lourens's lip trembled, and his eyes swelled with tears, but he did not cry. In exchange for our silence, Kagiso put his brawn to work in service of our vision.

The walls were made of corrugated iron, which we were forbidden from touching lest we cut ourselves, contract tetanus and suffer the same fate as our doomed Aunt Daphne.

But looking at him now I realised Lourens was a stranger

to me. Apparently he was learning to play the electric guitar. 'An extravagance,' my mother said, 'for a child that age.' This was the boy who forced members of the gang to defecate in our specially made gang toilet.

'A den must have a toilet,' he reasoned, 'otherwise it's not like a proper house.' While a boy squatted my cousin poked him in the bottom with a stick so that he leapt to his feet and smeared his legs with shit. This trick made us laugh. That was the good thing about Lourens. He did things you would never dare, like build dens, blackmail the gardener and poke boys in the bottom with sticks. We had shared memories of the strange perversity of childhood, the obsession with excrement, the first understanding of sex and erections. But this was not enough to bridge the gap between the two of us, one adolescent, the other on the cusp. We regarded each other with distrust and inexplicable loathing.

My aunt stood with her son. Her red hair was pulled back and piled on her head like a bird's nest. Her glasses with thick black frames sat far down on her nose. I liked her very much, but for reasons then unknown to me, my mother and father were strongly opposed to the woman. Though I liked *You Magazine* with its hook-for-hand-boys, it was still vulgar, because my parents said so. And even if I harboured a secret admiration for people such as Savimbi and my aunt, my parents' judgement stood, for they were my parents.

That Ouma, who had kept this family in uneasy orbit, had gone supernova in the furnace was evidenced by the patchy clusters of people seated in the plastic chairs of Sunnyvale Retirement Home. Already they were splintered. I wondered about my inheritance. Ouma had promised me all the books but they were nowhere to be seen. Were they supposed to present them here? Was there supposed to be some sort of ceremony in which the minister called people up and presented them with Ouma's leftover things? That would be a good way to do it. Perhaps someone else had taken the books, but if it came to it, I could call my parents, as witnesses. My grandmother had told me, *in front* of my parents, that those books were *mine*. Ouma said so and now, dead, Ouma was as good as God.

The poisonous dwarf cleared his throat and everyone was silent so that he could talk briefly and unimaginatively about an old woman cavorting with God. I relished my family's distaste for the man. That was what I loved about these Afrikaners, my Afrikaners. They were so hard and unforgiving. They would not let the poisonous dwarf out of the room unscathed by their radiating distaste. The professor got to his feet and though he was large and powerfully built, a former athlete, before the family he looked unsteady and nervous. I knew my uncle drank a lot. My whole family drank a lot. We loved alcohol. We weren't alcoholics. We drank the Afrikaner way which was really like taking medicine. You drank to fortify yourself. Alcohol did not break up our family, alcohol brought it together. Alcohol was amazing stuff; was alchemy. What else could transform grief into sweet melancholy? How extraordinary the discovery that your state of mind was nothing but a function of the molecules circulating in your bloodstream! My uncle and his wife drank lots of gin martinis, very dry gin martinis in proper martini glasses, from about noon onwards and by nine or ten that night, stumbling only a little, they found they quite liked each other.

On the morning of Ouma's funeral all the adults in attendance knew that the physicist and his wife had been drinking a lot. He said, 'Our mother's life was not a particularly happy one. Her life was largely bitter. She had a few consolations. Her children have succeeded, more or less. We have prospered to a greater or lesser degree.'

One had to wonder about these Afrikaners – one had to wonder what the hell they had to be so bitter about. Setting aside the fact that he grew up poor and that his father gassed himself and that a few siblings died, he didn't have an altogether horrible adulthood, which was not without some success. South Africa did not come without its costs. Now that they were rich and powerful, why did they not indulge in the jolly excesses the English colonials seemed so capable of? Why were they always so fucking miserable? But my stubborn uncle, who liked putting people to death, could see our way of life slipping away. His mother's life was not much of a stake in the ground, and neither was his. The university was becoming bilingual. His daughter, a once bright and vivacious woman, had become a missionary and moved with her feckless husband to Bethlehem, in the middle of the Karoo. His nephews could no longer speak Afrikaans and his sisters bought them electric guitars. In the din of everyday life he must have made out the air-raid siren calling for a quick evacuation. Like mistreated dogs, the Afrikaners snarled and snapped and then, tail between legs, slouched towards Bethlehem, a godforsaken town at the end of a worthless continent.

He continued:

'She was a good woman, a God-fearing woman. She lived a hard life in order to clothe and feed us. And I loved her and I am very grateful to her.'

And with that he stopped and walked back to his chair. I saw that he was crying. Grief was indeed so powerful that it compelled my uncle to stand up and say something, however faltering or meaningless, to flail against the unhappiness. I made a note of this. This counted against the Afrikaners. The English, they were less sentimental. It was very embarrassing to see such a large Boer cry. We left the building and noticed that the air was thick with flying ants. When we got home there would be dead flying ants in the shallow pools of water in the bath and dead flying ants in cold cups of tea, left standing on kitchen counters.

9

The God catcher

MRS HENNINGS SAID, 'Gerhard Moerdyk is South Africa's greatest architect. He designed the Voortrekker Monument.' Mr Moerdyk undertook the complex calculations, the detailed designs necessary to ensure that every year, at twelve noon, on 16 December, the sun shone through the opening of the monument's dome on to a cenotaph which read, *We for thee, South Africa*, to commemorate that day when history and God came together, when the rivers ran red with blood and the Afrikaners decided that He was on their side after all. The Voortrekker Monument was the coming together of mathematics and culture. It delivered a moment of superlative kitsch that drew Boers from around the country who wanted to see for themselves their God made manifest.

God was big in Africa. He was big with the blacks and He was big with the whites and there was no escaping Him. It was impossible not to be a little religious when your history teacher crammed you into a bus and drove you to the Voortrekker Monument so that she could declare, 'Behold – the Boers, the greatest people on earth, have built a God catcher!' And every year, sure enough, He turned up and by shining bright on that cenotaph said, 'Carry on as you mean to.' God was in Pretoria. He was in the Voortrekker Monument and the Union buildings and in the streets wide enough for our holy ox-wagons.

I never really gave much thought to the Church of England God who must surely have existed for me culturally, if not theologically. He was a nice God. He didn't care if you divorced people, or cremated them. He didn't care if you ate pig and He really wouldn't be so rude as to have an opinion about where you stuck your willy (even if it happened to be inside a shampoo bottle). The Church of England God had, as his representative in the promised land, Archbishop Desmond Tutu, which revealed impeccable taste; he was a man of good humour and admirable political convictions. This was a God who would have good reason to be mad at me for being a blaspheming little pervert – but would still forgive me because He was such an all-round nice guy, like Father Christmas. But the problem with the English God was that all the things that made Him really likeable, all the things that actually made His existence tolerable, were also the things that made Him such a wimp, such a poofda, such an outright bloody *moffie* that He didn't stand a hope in hell against the Dutch Reformed God, against the strapping God with big tanned hairy forearms, the God with the enormous cock who was everywhere and showed up once a year to say, 'Carry on as you mean to.' Even in heaven the Afrikaners were wiping the floor with us.

The drivers of the Paul van Jaarsveld buses, in their shorts and knee-high socks, with their thick moustaches, looked so alike that for a long time I thought our driver was the eponymous Paul van Jaarsveld himself; an enterprising man who bought a bus and made a living from school tours. The drivers were working-class Afrikaners and we laughed at their accents. Their severely parted hair shone with Brylcreem and after a long day of driving they would retire to their homes in the poor suburbs of Pretoria West.

Trips to the Voortrekker Monument invariably included a visit to the Natural History Museum. The only exhibit of real interest was a life-size re-creation of a caveman being attacked by a sabre-toothed tiger. Another tiger was dragging a child away by its skull. One of its teeth had pierced the infant through the eye and the child's hair was matted with blood. The caveman's penis was visible beneath thick hair covering his body, as were the breasts of his 'wife'. There was much to delight in at this exhibit so we lingered for a long time. The caveman had a very big penis and his wife very hairy breasts. Some child, I don't know whether to provoke or out of genuine curiosity, asked whether this couple was Adam and Eve, to which our science teacher Miss Jewel snapped, 'Most certainly not.' Aaron daringly touched the woman's breasts when Miss Jewel's back was turned which made the girls squeal. Miss Jewel said, 'Girls – stop being so ridiculous!'

In the display about waterborne diseases I learnt that it is impossible to contract bilharzia merely by urinating in water. When Emmanuel caught me taking a leak into a storm-water drain, he said, 'You'll get bilharzia if you do that. They'll swim up your pee and into your willy.' I put my dick back into my pants so fast that I wet my safari suit and got my foreskin caught in the zipper. Even the cleverest boy in school got some facts wrong.

I don't want to ascribe too much cunning to our teachers and our school and the government and all that, but really there was no better place to take children than the Natural History Museum if you wanted to drive home the point that your survival was almost entirely dependent on the suffering of some other innocent creature. The Natural History Museum taught us that life is an economy of suffering so that when we die, like my grandmother, we are an accumulation of those compromises, bones and loose skin, mildly anti-Semitic, mildly racist, nothing rampant or unseemly, having suffered and caused suffering, dying, I suppose, with a small credit but completely ravaged by all the exchanges.

Of course, I am not saying as stupid eleven-year-olds we understood this explicitly, but we probably understood something of this when we first saw that child as the meal of a sabre-toothed tiger. For want of fancy interactive exhibits and video screens and everything else that constitutes the theme-parked ghastliness of modern institutions, the museum made up for it with tacky but enthralling scenes of pain and suffering from the natural world which gave it an existential quality I imagine Schopenhauer would have admired.

When the trips were finished, Paul van Jaarsveld drove us to the Union buildings where we sat on the president's lawn and ate our packed lunches while, for all we knew, he watched us and gave instructions to build the bomb in Afrikaans.

Emmanuel, Aaron and I collected the leftover lunches, waited for Thomas to fall asleep and pelted his face with tuna sandwiches, sticky side out, until, enraged, fat fists flying like an enormous newborn, he tried to avenge himself.

'Thomas – stop being so ridiculous!' said Miss Jewel.

* * *

Petrus was very annoyed that I hadn't told him about the trip to Pretoria because he had waited for me to walk home with him after school.

'Why didn't you tell me?'

'I forgot,' I said.

'I waited and waited.'

'I'm sorry.'

'Letsatsi robbed us on Sunday.' This was why he had waited for over an hour.

'What?'

'She robbed us and ran away.'

'With a gun?'

'No – while we were at church.'

'How do you know it was Letsatsi?'

'Because she was supposed to be making lunch. And then when we came back she was gone. My mother called the police. They came to the house. She called Letsatsi a bitch. She even stole the krugerrands.' I could see how this would be a blow. Those tacky gold medallions were Tannie Vera's pride and joy. In sufficient number they may even have been part of her retirement plan.

'And when the police came my mother said, "That woman is an ungrateful *bitch*."'

The police were apparently hosted in the formal sitting room with the grey leather recliners. His mother served two packets of Romany Creams and filter coffee. They were very polite and commiserated with the loss of kruger-rands – who would not? – but said there was only a small chance of ever finding Letsatsi if she had fled to Zimbabwe as Tannie Vera suspected. As a last resort, she called the building society to enquire whether Letsatsi had an account. It was a complex business, her identity only confirmed when Tannie Vera said, 'Ag, you know, the *bad-tempered* one,' whereupon she was immediately informed that Letsatsi had withdrawn all her savings with, for the first time ever, 'a big bantu smile. All teeth and pink lips.'

'One time,' Petrus said, 'when Letsatsi didn't want to work, she said her uncle died and she had to go to Zimbabwe. That's why my mother thinks she's in Zimbabwe. But my mother said that blacks have so many aunts and uncles that you can't keep track. She says the blacks are always at this funeral or that funeral. She says with the blacks that even if the mother of your sister of your cousin twice removed died they will go to the funeral. Do you think Letsatsi is in Zimbabwe?'

'Zimbabwe has a black president,' I said.

'Yes,' Petrus responded, 'my father says he's a communist.'

'Not all black presidents are communists.'

I was not sure about this. The relationship between black politics and communism was something that eluded me. The illustrated book about sex was missing too. I argued it was unlikely that Letsatsi would have taken it but Petrus insisted that he searched the house and there was no sign of the book. I imagined Letsatsi in her purple blouse and dark skirt, sitting in the back of a blue Putco bus, suitcase strapped to the roof, stuffed with clothes, krugerrands and the *Illustrated Married Couple's Guide to Better Love Making*, illegally imported from Lesotho.

Petrus said there was no need for us to be concerned about Susie because 'she's a good black'. It was a common phrase. On the whole, Petrus chose his words carefully. He had no feelings about race or politics. He simply delighted in the world of adults and reported all the things overheard in his household. When he said, 'Susie is a good black,' he wanted to assure me that in spite of what had happened, he understood that I had a special relationship with her. It would always put her above suspicion. He too was fond of Susie and he wanted to be worthy of my family that looked down on his. In any event, an enlightened view was more sophisticated. He could not imagine people travelling first class on South African Airways ever using the word 'bantu', let alone 'kaffir'. He correctly intuited that the right political attitude was a matter of class. He even understood that the right political attitude had very little to with the right political action. But when he said that Susie was a good black, I got angry, not because the comment was offensive in a way ordinarily understood, but because I grasped a deeper and more disturbing meaning. It bothered me for a long time. It bothered me many years after they unbanned the ANC and many years after a new government was formed. It bothered me after Mugabe went mad – 'He's got syphilis,' they said, 'everyone knows he fucks like a rabbit' – and after Mad Mugabe destroyed his country and all the whites started saying, 'You see, that's Africa for you.' It bothered me because Letsatsi on a blue Putco Bus was a magnificent vision of someone who had singularly defied the odds, who had done something brave and heroic, like Winnie Mandela, that huge hulking presence of a woman, who also went mad, fist in the air rallying her supporters. Letsatsi on the bus, like Jonas Savimbi with his red beret, who died with bullet wounds to the head, pictures of which I would see printed in the newspaper. When Petrus said, 'Susie is a good black,' there was a sense that I and my family were more deeply implicated in this strange country than Petrus and his lower-middle-class, gun-toting, *You Magazine*-reading family, who had driven their maid to an act of beautiful rebellion and freedom from the strange netherworld in which the maid shuffled between her room and the kitchen, in which her entire existence could be spent as the stage-hand of an utterly dreary domestic drama in which not very much happened to not very interesting people. And this sense of unease was only deepened by Percy. I hated him for reminding me that Susie was really not part of my family and that she didn't stay with us because she loved me, because she was my second mother. She stayed with us because it was her job. Like Letsatsi, Susie probably also wanted to go home. Home was not in Linden or Johannesburg. Home was in Kabalazani or Lesotho or where she could be with her family. And I wondered if Susie would be jealous of Letsatsi, for saying, finally, enough is enough. I was frightened that one day Susie would too. She would turn to me and my family and say, 'Enough is enough. I'm going home.' So when Petrus said, 'Susie is a good black,' I turned to him and said, 'Don't say that. That's an awful thing to say. The reason she stole your stuff was because you only gave her a zinc bath. If you had given her a nice bath and you were nice to her she wouldn't have left. You deserved it.' Petrus was so angry that he left without saying a word. It was Friday and he was going to spend the night, but I spoilt every-thing with my outburst.

That evening I sulked. Lisa had come home for the weekend but there was no chance of Rorschach cards or anything fun because she had invited Nicola over and they stood in the kitchen with my parents talking about university and drinking wine. I was told to 'entertain myself'. After dinner, Lisa and Nicola went up to my sister's room so that they could catch up about their new lives and politics and boys and Nicola's alcoholic parents and sit in her room and smoke and drink. Since Lisa had gone to university we didn't fight in quite the same way any more. She would just roll her eyes and say things like. 'Jack, behave' or 'That's enough of that' or 'Oh, do keep quiet', as if she were my mother, which irritated me but was probably better than those painful back slaps she was so good at. It was different now that Lisa and Nicola were grown up. When they were young I was sometimes allowed to play a bit part in their games. In their favourite, 'Showjumping and Horse-riding School', I was permitted to be the jump.

'All right,' Nicola used to say, 'I'll be Gonda Beatrix and you can be the jump.'

'When can I be Gonda Beatrix?'

'You're a boy. Now get down or my horse will trample you. And then he'll be lame and I'll have to shoot him with my pistol.'

But now my sister was only interested in horses if there was a threat of them being turned into glue, and Nicola (even though she looked like a horse) was only interested in being a lesbian like my Auntie Pam, who wasn't my auntie, but was a lesbian, though I didn't know what this meant. From what I could gather, being a lesbian had a lot to do with going to Wits University which was full of radicals and hippies and people who didn't want to go to the army, which I thought was fair enough because I didn't have any desire to go the army, though my parents said I would probably have to. If I did go to the army they said I should become a navy diver to keep me out of the townships or away from the border. Being a navy diver was a way of being in the army without it being political. And though I agreed whenever the issue of conscription was raised, I had secretly hatched a plan *not* to be a navy diver, because I could think of few things more horrifying than being lowered into the shark-infested inky blackness to weld things or look for bodies in raging torrents. I would instead learn to play an instrument, possibly the drums or the triangle or something that didn't require too much effort or too much talent, and play in the navy band instead. Of course this would be a little embarrassing. I'm sure my parents would have preferred to say of their son 'He's a navy diver' than 'He's a navy percussionist' but it wasn't as if they had to dive in the harbour. My main fear was that I would be welding one of the giant propellers and someone would switch the engines on and I'd be sucked into the whirring blades. I suppose these sorts of considerations occupied the students at Wits too, for they only had another two or three years to figure out how they would *not* go the army or, if they had to, how to go into the army in the least inconvenient and distasteful and dangerous way. But the fact that Nicola was a lesbian also had something to do with being in the art department and her lecturer who apparently had a great reputation for turning all young girls into lesbians or Marxists and sometimes, when all the planets and the stars were in alignment, into Marxist lesbians. These were the sorts of things that apparently happened at Wits University and to a lesser extent at UCT, because everyone in Johannesburg knew that people in Cape Town were lazy and it took effort to be a Marxist. Because of all these facts, Nicola, who slapped me round a great deal less, held a new fascination for me, even though my parents sometimes rolled their eyes when my sister spoke of Nicola's 'political and sexual awakening'. This phrase caught my attention: a sexual awakening. This was something distinct from puberty because Nicola had had big floppy breasts for almost as long as I could remember. Nicola's sexual awakening was something worth investigating.

When I went to bed that night, I noticed the door was ajar and I peered into my sister's room. I could see the flickering of candles even though my parents had told her that it was stupid and dangerous on account of the wooden shingle roof. But my sister said what was stupid and dangerous was living in a room made of asbestos and that she'd rather die in a fire than of asbestosis and my mother said, 'Lisa, stop being so silly. You are not to light candles in your bedroom,' but my sister did it anyway.

Standing on the floor was an open bottle of red wine, an overflowing ashtray and my sister's old tape deck. My sister sat on the floor cross-legged and sipped her wine. Nicola was lying on the bed, naked. She'd propped herself up with two continental pillows and blew smoke out the window. This was the first time I'd seen a vagina that did not belong to a member of my family. Nicola had a thick bush of pubic hair and it looked like it was moving in the breeze but that might have been my imagination. Reclined on the bed with a cigarette in her hand, that great big hairy mound between her legs, she looked, for the first time, quite beautiful, and I was astonished. But that night, when I *skommelled*, I thought about the hairs growing from Nicola's ugly birthmark on the side of her face, and how these hairs were like her pubic thatch and how they also moved in the breeze like grass. And I thought again about Ouma and what she would make of me masturbating and how, in any case, she probably knew, she was probably watching. But mostly I thought about Percy and how he would laugh at me. I could hear him giggling. Oh Nicola, oh Amie, oh Chad, oh Chad, oh Chad! You are a dirty boy. This is a funny beez-nus. And it made me angry again and I thought about how much I hated Percy.

* * *

My mother's highest form of condemnation, her most severe sanction of an action, would be to describe it as 'unforgivable'. When I hit my sister over the head with an All Gold tomato sauce bottle she said it was 'very naughty'. When she caught me stealing money out of her purse she said it was 'very, very naughty'. When I disowned fat Thomas Baird for being too fat she said it was 'mean-spirited, selfish, shallow, stupid and cruel'. When I burnt ants with a magnifying glass she said it was 'beastly and horrible'. When I threw the cat in the swimming pool to see if it could swim (it couldn't) she said I was an 'evil child'. But she had never used the word 'unforgivable' in respect of anything I had done – nor did I believe she ever would. Not because I considered myself incapable of real cruelty or evil – I knew I was capable of a great many cruel and depraved things – but because I thought myself too small, too weak to be capable of grand action, of genocide or mass murder, of anything significant enough to warrant this sanction.

It was a sweltering week in Johannesburg. It hadn't rained for weeks and the grass had turned a patchy brown. I lazed in front of the television.

'You'll get square eyes if you sit in front of the TV all day,' my mother said.

'I won't.'

'Why don't you go for a swim?'

'Don't feel like it.'

'Don't be silly. Of course you feel like a swim. Come on – get outside.'

'But Percy's there.'

'So?' my mother said.

'I don't like swimming when Percy's there.'

'Why?'

'Because.'

'Because what?' she snapped.

'He's always . . . *looking* at me.'

'What do you mean, looking at you?'

'He's always staring at me.'

'So?'

'He was looking at me when I was changing the other day,' I said, before adding, 'He's gross.'

'Do you mean while you were naked?'

'Yes.'

'Did he do anything?'

'No.'

'Why were you naked?'

'I was just changing at the pool.'

She paused for a moment. 'I think you're being very silly.'

I knew, I knew deep down, that this small thing I did to Percy, almost inconsequential, but then again not, was unforgivable. Later, much later, when I spoke to Susie and she said, 'The people at the church, they say to me, Susie, you mustn't worry. Who is this white boy Jack? He is your son. God He replace. He replace my baby. God He give me a new son. God He give me a better son,' I felt sick because I didn't know what to say. I didn't even know what shape my confession could take. The next day, Percy was gone. 'Don't worry,' my mother said, 'I didn't tell Susie anything. I just said it was best for him to leave.' At the time I felt a little guilty, but I told myself that it was better for everyone. Percy stood a far better chance of going to school if he lived with his father. Perhaps what I had done was a little cruel, but the ends justified the means. Everyone would be happier this way. To make myself feel better, I took a renewed interest in Percy's welfare.

'How's Percy?' I asked. Susie looked at me suspiciously.

'Why?'

'Oh, I just want to know. It was nice when he sat at the pool.'

'But you fight with Percy.'

'Oh – just that one time. It was my fault.'

'What Percy do that time?'

I was sorry I had asked now.

'He pushed me in the pool,' I said.

'Why you get so cross?'

'Because I hurt myself. I hit my elbow. On the ledge. And I shouted at him. I'm sorry about that. It was rude.'

'Ai – something else. There is something you are not telling me. I can see it in your face.'

'No – there's nothing. I'm going to watch TV.'

'Jack!' I turned round to look at her. 'I can see it in your face, my boy. I have eyes.'

I considered my parents' judgement in all things perfect. This was not a delusion they suffered from. It was entirely my own. Any casual or flippant remarks, though forgotten by them, left an ineradicable mark on my mind like a branding iron. Does one not outgrow one's parents' opinions? But blind, absolute admiration for their perfect aesthetic and moral judgement had somehow to reconcile itself with circumstances that were indisputably compromising. It was a problem to grow up in a country in which everything was so perverted, even if you had the right political attitude, even if you were inclined towards the right political action.

I fought with my parents, in particular my father, because he could be very, very prickly. He was, for instance, the most uncompromising man in the world when it came to table manners. He was locked in a protracted battle with Rachel about the correct way in which to hold her knife and fork. And like most people who grew up poor but went on to make some money, he could not escape the notion that he had done a disservice to his children by not giving them an opportunity to grow up poor too, so that they could appreciate the value of money. He couldn't abide cheekiness, or rudeness or most especially sullenness. There was nothing worse than a child that sulked. So sometimes he raged at his children. Other times he raged at his cars because he had a taste for terribly impractical models like the old army jeep that was made entirely of metal, including the seats, and a battered yellow MG and a Volkswagen Kombi that had been converted into a 4X4 by an enterprising Indian mechanic who had a shop in downtown Johannesburg. All these impractical cars that he had such a fondness for would overheat and break down, sometimes in the middle of the Karoo, or the Free State, or the Transkei and then we'd have to sit in the car and wait while he and my mother set off on foot to get help and we'd be miserable because there is no longer hour than the hour sitting in a car, in the Karoo, in the heat, with nothing to do and no sense of how long you would have to wait until your parents returned. So my father would rage at these cars. He would kick the tyres and bumpers and roar with anger, but if ever we suggested that he might like to consider a normal car like everyone else, he would look upset because he couldn't understand why his children didn't have any sense of adventure.

So there were lots of things in the world that aggravated my father but if I had to put a finger on what it was that made him a little prickly, there were a great many things I would need to consider, such as all those dead siblings and the suicidal axe-wielding father and living in a hostel and having the matron for your mother – all these things must have played a part in his general prickliness, but of course this was not all, or even nearly all.

Within my father there were two complementary impulses: a breathtaking, wounding cynicism together with an enormous capacity for forgiveness. His mind always settled upon the most unflattering, the most ignominious explanation for the difficulty you found yourself in and then he forgave you for it. In this respect he was the perfect candidate for the law. I never knew whether this nature was what led him to the law in the first place or whether, faced with a succession of greedy and jealous and depraved individuals, he inadvertently shaped himself when he settled upon a respectable profession as the easiest way out of Krugersdorp and that horrible pile of dead babies and bitter Afrikaners.

Whatever the answer, our household was infused with the law, and the holy of holies was my father's chambers on Pritchard Street in the centre of Johannesburg. Through two oak doors of the reception area where his secretary sat, you entered into a vast, book-lined space with a consulting table that seated twelve people. I believed there was nothing so bad that you could do, for which my father, sitting here with his books and his papers, could not devise an exit strategy. In here, at this table, there could be forgiveness and salvation. There was of course the problem of Joseph Mabena, the man who chopped women up with a machete, and we knew of course that what happened to Joseph Mabena still worried my father very much, *but he did chop those women up with a machete*. He cheerfully admitted to doing this and there wasn't really forgiveness for him, because they still hanged him, but maybe there was salvation because the judge did say, he must have said, 'May the Lord have mercy upon your soul,' because if he didn't say that, it wouldn't have been legal and they wouldn't have been able to hang him. Perhaps there couldn't always be forgiveness *and* salvation. But you'd have to do something pretty bad, something pretty consequential, for there not to be.

In the evenings, after my father had had a few drinks, a kind of melancholy, confessional, conspiratorial mood would take hold of him. If you were not in the mood for talking, then you'd yawn and make your excuses – but if you were, then you'd stick around and see where the evening took you. It required alcohol, specifically J&B whisky, administered in two-finger doses – not, as my father would say, 'skinny-finger doses' but large meaty Boer-hand doses – no water, no ice. And then there would be music played on his Linn Sondek turntable, of which he was immensely proud. He said to me, 'Jack, I think we should move to America. Who wants to live in this awful country? Perhaps we should live in New York. Wouldn't that be marvellous? We could all live in an apartment in New York and eat bagels for breakfast.' Suddenly energised, he jumped up to look for his Neil Diamond record and played 'Coming to America' so loudly that the panes in the window frames vibrated. America, for all its faults, was the moneyed, glorious, shining rebuke to everything that filthy, benighted South Africa had become. These were the sorts of things that would happen on those special evenings when a particular combination of alcohol and music would create a mirage, which could only be sustained for a short time; by morning it had faded away. When I was young I believed him when he said these things and I would go to school and tell my friends, 'We're moving to

America – we're going to live in New York and eat bagels,' and at first my friends would believe me but after a while I had to insist, 'No, this time it's true.'

In addition to the dead siblings and poverty and lunatic father and the general *misery* of being Afrikaans, there was helplessness *and* complicity, which germinated deep within and sprouted as delicate harmless prickles. I did not know what my father would have said about what I did to Percy. I wondered whether all boys wanted the approval of their fathers. Did one still need it when one was able to shoot jets of come, in and over all manner of people? Did one still need it when one was a man, a man as much as Anton?

It was my father who introduced me to the word 'philosophy'. I was quite young at the time, perhaps not much older than six or seven. He said it was about good and evil and why we were alive and whether there was a God and a devil.

'Philosophers,' he said, 'tell us how we should live our lives.'

'Why?'

'Because that's their job.'

'Do they tell people what they *have* to do?' I asked.

'No,' my father said. '*Dictators* tell people what they *have* to do. Philosophers tell us what we *should* do.'

'So you have to listen to a dictator but you don't have to listen to a philosopher?'

'Yes – but I think you're missing the point.'

'Why?'

'Because it's not all about telling people what to do.'

'So is it better to be a dictator or a philosopher?'

'It's better to be a philosopher.'

'Why?'

'Because most dictators end up dead.'

'Why?'

'Because they make people unhappy and people don't like them.'

'Is P.W. Botha a dictator?'

'No – he's a president.'

'Is Savimbi a dictator?'

'No – he's a terrorist.'

'Is Ronald Reagan a dictator?'

'No – he's a president.'

'Is the Queen a dictator?'

'No – she's the Queen.'

'So who is a dictator?'

'Hitler.'

'Who are *alive* dictators?'

'Castro and Gaddafi.'

'Is someone going to kill them?'

'I don't know.'

'Should someone kill them?'

'No.'

'Why?'

'You shouldn't kill anyone.'

'Not even dictators?'

'No.'

'Not even Hitler?'

'That's a very philosophical question.'

'Why?'

'Because that's the thing philosophers talk about.'

'About killing dictators?'

'Yes.'

'Is it the philosophers that kill dictators?'

'In a way, I suppose.'

'How?'

My father could only indulge the inexorable idiocy of a child for so long. 'With swords.'

'You're lying.'

'I'm not. All philosophers have light sabres.'

'Like Luke Skywalker?'

'Like Luke Skywalker.'

'Where do they get them?'

'From the university.'

'Green ones or red ones?'

'Green ones.'

I wonder if, when at the age of seventeen I informed my parents that I would be studying philosophy, my father finally regretted having associated that particular cultural touchstone with such a limited and limiting field of study. Neither my passion for *Star Wars* nor philosophy waned during my adolescence (though the former remained a secret thanks to my highly developed instinct for self-preservation).

For a long time I thought I would be a philosopher too. To be a philosopher seemed to me the noblest calling in the world. But as I progressed through university accumulating degrees, there came a point during which I saw, for the first time, the vast ocean of gall that existed between the assignations 'philosopher' and 'academic'. A person of modest abilities recognised that it was not an ocean they cared to be seen paddling in. But what better way to atone for past transgressions than appointing yourself a moral arbiter?

At first, not knowing what happened at the pool, she was reluctant to talk to me, but towards the end of the year Susie revealed that all was not well at home.

'He is causing big trouble that one. His father he phone

me and say he find the carton. One carton of Chesterfield. Where he get the money for this, Jack? Smoking is too expensive. And his father he say he think Percy is drinking. Me, Jack, I don't like the beers. When people drink I don't like. I say to him, "Percy, are you drinking?" He say to me, "No, Mama, I'm not drinking." I say to him, "Is your father a liar?" Ai – that one – I don't know what to do with him. You think he's drinking, Jack?' I shrugged. Susie put the iron down and wiped her forehead with a handkerchief. I didn't like these conversations any more. It was important that Percy did well, that everything worked out for the best. If things were not going well I didn't want to hear about it.

'Don't worry about it, Suz,' I said. 'I know lots of boys in high school drink beers. It doesn't mean they're tsotsis.'

'Who drinks beer?'

'Boys – in high school.'

'Your friends?'

'No – not my friends. Like . . . you know . . . people's brothers. Like Anton.'

'Anton is not in high school. Anton is a man. He is a big guy – he was in the army. Jack – you are too young to drink. If I catch you – there will be big trouble.'

'I know, Susie. I don't even like beer.'

'How do you know? You are such a little kid – how do you know?'

'I tasted it once.'

'What? When?'

'My dad let me try. It's horrible. I'll never drink. I don't like it. And my mom let me try wine once. I thought it would taste like grape juice – but it was sour.'

'Ja. That's good.'

'I was just saying that maybe if he has a beer – it's not too bad. And lots of people in high school smoke. My dad smokes and Anton smokes. Oom Frik smokes. Everyone smokes.'

'It's too expensive. He is not working! He has no money. I give him money. His father give him money. I do not work to buy this one cigarettes. I do not wash your dirty clothes to buy him cigarettes and beers. I do not clean your toilet so this one can get drunk.'

'Do you not like it here?' I said sullenly.

'I like it here. I like. But what your mommy say? Money doesn't grow on trees. I like this thing. It's true. Money does not grow on trees. And I worry, Jack – his father is very strict. What happens if his father say to him he must go? Where he stay? His granny – my mother – she say she is finish with this one. Yo yo yo, Jack – she was angry with him. She say he is very badly behaved.'

'Well, he's going to go to school next year. And then he will get a matric.'

'Ja – we will see. I go and talk to the principal. She is a nice lady. She say she will make the exception. She say he can go standard eight – if he work hard. When I tell Percy he was so happy. He was dancing. It's all right this way. I don't want he only get the matric when he is an old man. The people will laugh at him. They will say – such an old guy and still in school! But about this I am very happy.'

Susie was beginning to look old and tired. There was a rip in her overalls beneath her left breast and I could make out the pattern of one of my mother's old T-shirts. Her hair was thinning. When I was a toddler I would pat her springy oiled air and sniff my hands and Susie would say, 'You like the Black-Like-Me? Yes, it smells nice.' She sighed more now. She had wrinkles by her eyes. Could it be that people actually age in bursts, that at some point during the night, the body, that's been holding on so tight, that's been fighting, just lets go for a second and loses some ground against the world, before steadying itself, pushing back and commencing battle once again?

That night, after Susie had said to me, 'I can see it in your face, my boy. I have eyes,' and I was feeling unsettled and guilty, I went to sit with my father in the lounge. He was listening to classical music and sipping whisky.

'Do you think Percy is going to be OK?' I asked him.

'What do you mean?' he asked.

'With his dad?'

'I don't know. I don't really know his dad.'

'Susie says he's a prince. But he works in the courthouse in Pretoria.'

'I know.'

'Do you like Percy?'

'I don't really know Percy very well, Jack. I think he's very angry. With good reason.'

'Because we sent him away?'

'That too.'

'Do you think he's right to be angry with us for sending him away?'

'Yes,' my father said. I swallowed. Did my father suspect me? I had heard people say that my father was a good lawyer. They said he was a good lawyer not because he knew the law but because he knew people. He said the best way to deal with things was just to tell the truth. He said that to the woman who murdered two people with a pair of scissors – the woman the press dubbed the 'Scissor Murderer' – but they didn't execute her because it was a *crime of passion*. And he must have said that to Joseph Mabena.

'Why?'

'Wouldn't *you* be angry, Jack? If someone sent you away from *your* mother? Or from me?'

'I suppose. But . . .'

'But?'

'I didn't . . . I didn't mean for Percy to be sent away.'

'Didn't you?'

'No . . . I . . . I don't know.' Could I just tell him? Would I feel better if I told him that what I said wasn't exactly true; that I had *misled* my mother? My father wasn't saying anything but he wasn't ending the conversation either. But I couldn't. I couldn't tell him what I was doing at the pool that day. I couldn't tell him about *skommelling* in the pool and I couldn't tell him about Amie and Chad. Could I say that I had *inadvertently* misled my mother? 'Inadvertently' was a very good word, perhaps even better than *megalomaniac*; it meant you'd made a mistake without thinking. If you walked out of a shop without paying for something you could just say, 'I'm sorry. I did that *inadvertently*,' which meant that you were daydreaming and not concentrating. This was different from not thinking about the consequences. Inadvertently meant *not thinking at all.* Of course, this was a lie too, but everyone knew there were some lies that were like little steps towards the truth. However, it was so difficult to take little steps with my father. If I just said the word 'inadvertently' he would know everything. You had to be very careful what you said to my father because he had an unpleasant habit of arriving at the truth almost instantly. He did not, unfortunately, have a blind spot where his children were concerned. Not like my mother. My mother couldn't be counted on to arrive at the truth. My mother was more charitable. And if my father did arrive at the truth, what would he say? He would forgive me. He would still love me. More than that! He would love me as much as a father could possibly love his son. But there would be a little part of me that would disgust him; a little part that I could never do anything about and that he would never forget. My father decided to end the conversation.

'Bedtime,' he said.

'OK,' I said without arguing. I wondered about this. I wondered whether he ended the conversation before I could say something that I couldn't take back. Perhaps, as a lawyer, he'd had his fill of unrelenting honesty. Maybe he sometimes wanted people to shut up and deal with things themselves.

10

The black mamba

THE LAST DAY of term always dragged in the English school. Our teacher continued with her lesson while I stared at the enormous pile of food beneath the blackboard. I felt ambivalent about the collection for cleaning and gardening staff; there would be that awkward moment during the end-of-term assembly when Mr Harrison would say, 'And now we would like to say a special thank you to our cleaning staff who keep our school beautiful,' and the cleaning staff, who had been waiting patiently outside the main doors of the hall, would walk on to the stage to receive their parcels. They would bend their knees and clap their hands like beggars receiving a coin. The children would stand and cheer.

All the pupils in the Afrikaans school gathered in the hall at 11 a.m. Wearied by three months of teaching, the staff ignored the boisterous behaviour of the assembled children as the senior boys opened the heavy velvet curtains with gold tassels and painstakingly lowered a cinema screen inch by inch for fear that they might further damage the tatty surface. The teachers walked around the hall drawing the curtains, while the children, scattered on the floor like heated corn kernels, twitched with excitement. Rumours circulated that this time the staff had selected a new film, one that had recently been screened at the local cinema. Without fail they managed to source one more of what seemed to be an interminable series of Bud Spencer and Terence Hill *skop-skiet-en-donner* (kick-shoot-and-fuck-up) films. We never suspected that the spaghetti westerns were not American, but Italian, or that Bud Spencer was in fact Carlo Pedersoli. Interest in what flickered a few feet above us quickly dwindled. Our chief entertainment was scooting undetected around the hall on our bums. By the end of the day, all semblance of discipline had broken down and even the most obedient were happily taking in the sights and sounds of the hall rarely seen and heard, like tourists in an unfamiliar city.

But in the English school there was no end-of-term film. They were decidedly lacking in those traditions that punctuated grey memories of schooldays that ran into one another with few discernible shapes. Those from an Afrikaans school would at least be able to say, 'Remember the terrible end-of-term flicks?' Indeed, I did not miss them. After an hour in the darkened hall with six hundred pupils, I would begin to feel claustrophobic and yearn to escape the muffled sound of the film, the airless heat of the hall, the noise of the school-children, and sprint home to begin the holidays.

In the winter months, Afrikaans families might spend a few weeks in the Kruger National Park, rising before dawn and queuing at the gates of the camp, hoping to be the first to enter the park. During the cool mornings, lions might stretch out on the tar roads thawing their limbs in the sun. But more often than not, hours would be spent in the dusty heat with nothing more diverting than impala and zebra.

Children would draw the home-made curtains in the Volkswagen kombi, lie back on the seat and sip their hot flat Coke while paging through comics, killing the hours before the mad rush back to the camp gates which closed at six o'clock. Those whose parents had grown up on farms or in the bushveld stood a better chance of seeing game. It took a sharp eye to spot a distant lion in the long grass or the ridged back of a crocodile in the river. The urbanised Afrikaner drove through the reserves, tired and hot, irritable with the bored children who longed to be home in front of television sets or at least playing with the other children in the camp pool. Their mythical connection to the land was sorely tested by a longing for the comforts of modern domesticity.

In the summer months people flocked to the seaside, to the warm waters of the south coast or the cool Atlantic Ocean of the Cape. Durban's gradual decline had been in evidence for a few years and so wealthier families bought holiday homes on the pristine beaches of Umhlanga, north of the city. Poorer families rented flats in Amanzimtoti further south. The morning after the schools closed, the roads were congested with large family cars, caravans and four-wheel drives towing motorboats. Petrol stations with Wimpy Bars and convenience stores were crowded with bad-tempered fathers and boisterous children making the seven-hour trek to the south coast or the twelve-hour trek to the Cape. Locals complained audibly about the invasion of the holidaymakers, who crowded their cities and drove badly. For a few weeks the interior of the country siphoned on to the beaches around the Republic: fishing, swimming, getting burnt, taking an invigorating drink of the land, fortifying themselves against the weariness that sometimes set in when they thought too long about what it took, and what it might still take, to keep all this to themselves.

Durban was full of snakes. My father's friend had a snake that lived in the postbox. The gardener killed it for them. It was a mean thing to do but the man's third wife said, 'It's too much to expect me to live with snakes in my postbox. We're not living in the bundus, you know.'

It was dark and cold so I pulled the blanket up over my shoulders. The drone and vibrations of the kombi on the motorway were soothing. My sister no longer came with us on holidays. At eighteen she said she was too old and that she'd rather spend the time with her friends in a house in Pilgrim's Rest – no doubt smoking marijuana and having sex, I thought. It was less fun without my sister. If she came along my father could be persuaded to flatten the seats and make a 'Christmas bed' in the back of the kombi. Occasionally the car strayed over on to green catseyes in the road and made a rhythmic clacking like a train, except duller, and I felt how my father guided the car to the centre of the road. The gentle motion and the rhythmic sounds lulled me into a pleasant state between sleep and wakefulness.

A few hours later my father pulled over to the side of the road. 'What's going on?' I asked.

'I saw something in the road,' he said. We all got out of the car.

'Stay here with your mother while I have a look.'

'Willem – for God's sake be careful,' my mother pleaded.

'Don't worry.'

My younger sister and I held my mother's hand.

'What the hell is your father up to?' she asked. In the middle of the motorway he bent down and picked up a large snake by its tail.

'Is it dead?' my sister asked.

'I think so,' my mother replied. But as my father walked back to the side of the road, the animal arched its back as if to strike. We all screamed and my father flung it away from his body.

'Idiot!' my mother yelled but my father just shrugged.

'Come and have a look,' he said.

We walked over to inspect the snake. 'Poor thing,' my father said. Its jaw was broken, torn away, and we could see the inside of its mouth. 'Heavens!' my mother said, 'That's a black mamba.' We all knew this because we had recently been to the snake park at Halfway House. The man at the snake park had squeezed the snake behind its head to show us. He said, 'These are dangerous snakes, hey – if they bite you, you can die in half an hour. You need to get some anti-venom quick.'

We walked back to the car, and while our backs were turned, my father struck its head with a rock to put it out of its misery. My father felt bad about everything. He felt bad about squashed snakes and three-legged dogs. He felt bad for spiders and told Susie to stop vacuuming their webs. He felt bad for stricken tortoises and stray cats and snails, which the gardener threw into a bucket of salt. In biology class it occurred to me that my father's grief knew no taxonomy; it spilt from kingdom, to phylum, to order, to family, to genera to species. For other people, normal people, these classifications were sluices that directed sympathy sparingly to a select few; but not my father. The sluices were overrun and his system was awash. People just shook their heads at this foolishness, for his sympathy was all well and good, but not when he did careless things like pick a black mamba up by its tail.

I thought about what had just happened. Specifically I

thought about parallel universes and how in some *other* universe that had up to this point been identical in every respect, from the crucifixion to the dastardly plotting of the KGB, my father had died, which set *that* universe upon a course quite different (in who knew what ways?) from our own. What, I wondered, as I lay in the car, would we have done if the snake had bitten my father? Waved down a passing car or driven him to the nearest town? Would we have sucked the venom from the bite? The man from the snake park told us this was very foolish. If the snake had bitten him, he probably would have died. He would have dropped the snake, clutched his heart and keeled over. Wham! And then I would have gone to school and said to Jürgen, 'My father died too. He was bitten by a black mamba.' *That* was a story. *That* was more interesting than cancer. *You Magazine* would have written an article about us. It would have included a photograph of me and my mother sitting on the settee in the living room. Looking at these pictures, people would have known that my family was different. We didn't have Van Gogh posters or dried flowers. Our settees weren't covered in soft grey leather nor were any of them recliners. But what would the people have said? I stared out the window and thought about this. People would have said, 'Silly fool for picking up a black mamba.' The delight in speculating about parallel universes, in which family members either did or did not die, lay in the fact that I, as their author, might, if the story took an unflattering twist, consider other alternatives.

It was a better story if I, not my father, got bitten by the snake, but certainly not through my own foolishness. In another universe I was innocently walking in the veld, when, out of nowhere, some aggrieved snake bit me. I had the presence of mind to strike the snake with a stone, not out of malice, but merely to confirm the species. The Kombi seat became a hospital gurney. A crowd of doctors and nurses ran along with me, shouting at astonished onlookers to clear the passage. I struggled to breathe as the doctors searched for a vein. They had seconds to inject the anti-venom. My forehead was clammy and my complexion pale. I remained calm, and though my breathing was laboured, I managed in a quiet voice to tell them what had happened. The doctors were astonished at the composure of one so young. I returned to school on crutches and when Jürgen asked what had happened, I said, 'I was bitten by a black mamba. I nearly died.'

We passed families who had pulled over at the designated picnic spots on the motorway; another deficiency of the Afrikaners. Petrus and his family also made *padkos* (road-food). Tannie Vera roasted a large packet of chicken drumsticks, made potato salad and milk tart, which she packed in Tupperware containers. Then the family stopped at one of the drab concreted squares a few metres from the road and sat down to lunch as if they were in the dining room at home. Petrus's father might even pray as the trucks on the N1 droned past. There were two flasks of coffee and two flasks of the wheeze-inducing orange juice. Some Afrikaners even stooped to warming food on the engine of the car. Potatoes wrapped in tinfoil were tucked between the greasy pistons and carburettors to bake as the car sped down the motorway.

After a few hours on the road we pulled off at one of the large petrol stations just outside of Harrismith.

'Oil and water, *baas*?' the attendant asked.

'No, thank you,' my father replied.

The attendant winked at me and I smiled back. A woman

with a bucket and squeegee washed the windscreen and my mother looked in her handbag for a fifty-cent coin. The woman stood by the car waiting until my mother opened the window and dropped the coin into her hands. She nodded a thank-you and walked to the next car but the man waved her away. As we ambled towards the restaurant, a man wearing shorts and a bright Hawaiian shirt opened the rear door of a four-wheel drive and helped his skinny maid out. The children ran after their mother and the maid leant against the car as she opened a container of pap and gravy. The man shook his head and pointed in the direction of a small grass clearing some way off. It was wrong to take your maid on holiday. Only selfish people did this. Still, it would have been nice if Susie came with us to the seaside. We could walk along the beach together and Susie could dip her feet into the sea while I went swimming. Black people loved seawater. Who didn't fill two-litre Coke bottles with seawater to take back home to their maids? What the water was used for remained a mystery. Some said they drank it or poured it in their baths. Others suggested that it was used for enemas. No matter; if Susie came along, she would have more seawater than any one woman would know what to do with. Also, there would be no arguments after dinner about who would wash the dishes.

The food in the Wimpy Bar was bad; the booths small and cramped; the service perfunctory. Diners wolfed down greasy breakfasts or tasteless burgers. Food spilt on to tables and mothers clutching paper serviettes mopped it up, beck-oned the waitress for more, and stacked empty plates and glasses at the edge of the table. They seemed like animals as they fell out of their cars, these large men and women, like cattle at a feeding trough. It was the mechanisation of feeding which brought into discomforting relief their bestiality.

I got up to go to the toilet and saw sitting behind us a man with his two children: a son aged about sixteen and a daughter my age. The rest of the diners looked like they had just stumbled out of bed, but father and son were freshly shaved. A faint blue shadow was discernible over their high cheekbones. They both wore clean white T-shirts and dark blue jeans. The girl, tomboyish, wore dungarees and sneakers. All of them had thick wavy black hair and glassy blue eyes. What struck me was how it was impossible to tell, just looking at them, whether they were English or Afrikaans. Usually, even if they didn't say a word, there would be some giveaway: the gait, the gestures or the features. It was not anything an anthropologist could describe; it was simply something a native could sense. Perhaps they were American? I had never seen an American, and anyway, what would Americans be doing in Harrismith? The town lay between Johannesburg and Durban. It was too far from anywhere to warrant even a snake park. It was the site of some important, but long-forgotten battles in the Anglo-Boer War. Nothing about Harrismith made it a likely place for me to learn about the arbitrary largesse of nature.

I walked to the bathroom and turned round to glance at them. The girl caught my eye. She smiled and I hurried through the bathroom doors. With some distaste I noticed that my feet were bare. The floor was sticky and I hoped that it was the detergent. I avoided the children's urinal even though, being short for my age, I found it more comfortable. The adult urinal was too close and the urine splashed back onto my stomach. I walked over to the basin and washed my hands. My shirt was stained and my uncombed hair stood wildly in all directions. I splashed my head with water, soaking the neck of my shirt as I pasted my hair to my forehead. I tried to dry myself with paper towels but a group of men came into the bathroom. I left before they reprimanded me for the mess. Feeling ridiculous, I walked around the other side of the restaurant, avoiding the family.

'What on earth have you been up to?' my mother asked.

'Nothing.'

'Why is your hair so wet?'

'I have a headache.'

'There are some tablets in the car.'

From where I was sitting I could still see them. The father and son smoked and waited for the girl to finish her strawberry milkshake. The absence of a mother, who (I decided) had died tragically, added a poignancy to the scene: marooned in obscene gluttony, peacocks in the pigsty.

For the remainder of the journey I lay on the seat of the car, smoking a pencil I found on the floor. My heart ached. It pained me that I would never see the family again. How did this happen? How was it that people so astonishing could momentarily step into the frame of your life, fill you with a bitter-sweet longing, only to disappear, ignorant of how they had been seared into your mind? Perhaps they were not ignorant. Perhaps they were sufficiently corrupted by their looks. And if they were not sufficiently corrupted there was always the influence of friends and family who would fawn and feed their vanity. Circumstance would gift them the ruthlessness required to maintain equanimity; otherwise, like Buddhist monks, they would develop a crippling and pathological aversion to harm. An aversion to harm might seem benign, but it could lead you to pick a black mamba up by its tail. Again the universe branched, and so that physics could remain physics, I, stricken, cradled in the arms of a man wearing jeans and a white T-shirt with his son and daughter on either side, made a path through the crowded hospital. 'Clear the way! This child has been bitten by a black mamba in the Wimpy Bar at Harrismith. Do clear the way!'

Indeed, it would take something catastrophic to create the unexpected and disruptive ripples in daily life required to bring me together with this unknown and unknowable family. But their memory lingered and I thought of the family often.

Soon the car was uncomfortably hot. I threw off the blanket and opened the window but the breeze was warm too. As we neared the coast it would become even hotter. That was the thing about Durban: the heat, the claustrophobic heat that prevented you from doing anything too quickly. Far better to sit in a deckchair fanning yourself beneath a white umbrella while those dark Indian waiters hovered about you, like flies at a bloated corpse. It stuck to you, cheap candyfloss and ice creams and sticky air and sticky sea. When you left Durban, there was a sticky, glistening string of Durban spittle that stuck to you.

I loved the beach. The Afrikaans families arrived early in the morning and erected a fortress. They stayed in the same spot all day and sometimes late into the night too. On the beach, you could stare at all the brown bodies: lithe Afrikaners with blue eyes, women with sagging breasts, men whose large penises could be made out through their tight costumes, boys with a 'V' of sun-bleached hair on the napes of their necks and girls my age with pronounced breasts.

My family spent hours at the beach each day. Sometimes, because of the formation of the sandbanks, large, powerful waves broke directly onshore. I would plant my feet firmly in the sand, and as the water rushed back into the sea it felt like I was moving at a hundred miles an hour across the surface of the planet.

Playing on the seashore I became lost in fantasies of my own making. When I was very young, my parents gave me a Kinder Surprise egg. Inside was a small orange parachutist. I played with him in the sand all day and then, balancing him on a plastic plate, took the toy into the ocean. A wave washed him away. I was frantic for the orange man and then, by some luck, caught sight of my toy a few metres away. It was extraordinary. What were the chances of finding the toy again in the vast ocean? We had been granted a reprieve. But ten minutes later I took him back into the ocean and I never saw the little orange man again. It pained me terribly. I had been given one lucky chance, but I blew it. The thought of that toy in the ocean made me sad and lonely.

My parents preferred to swim further out, past the breakers where the water was calmer. Sometimes they swam as far as the shark nets. Swimming by the shark nets made me uneasy. I imagined on the other side of the buoy a school of sharks, lying in wait for an unsuspecting swimmer who might easily be swept across the nets by a sudden swell. A shark caught in the nets, enraged, might thrash and bite off my foot. Swimming by the shark nets was asking for trouble. It was tempting the universe. But I wanted to show my parents and all those on the beach that I was a strong swimmer, that I was not afraid of the vast ocean or sharks and would go out much further than most people ever dared. When I got tired and started whining, my parents told me to swim back to shore. But I was too scared. Alone, in the open water, I was exposed. I imagined the sharks swimming just beneath me, and the horror of a dorsal fin breaking the surface without a parent present, to do what parents ought to: sacrifice themselves in case of the worst, offer their own limbs as I paddled safely to shore. So I waited, until my parents had had enough and decided to swim back to the beach and read their newspapers in the sun.

My mother liked holidays in Durban because it was where she was from. Her father worked for the railways and her mother was an inspector for the Indian schools. In Durban she acted younger and sometimes seemed quite girlish. She loved the trees filled with Indian mynahs even though Rachel and I clapped our hands over our ears because the noise they made was painful and deafening. She stole a long stick of sugar cane from a farm and chewed on it for hours while reading her book. She loved pawpaws and mangoes and bananas and lychees. We'd buy boxes of fruit from people selling them at the traffic lights and my mother would make mountains of lychee peels as she popped one piece of the fruit into her mouth after the other. Whenever we went to Durban we'd drive past Durban Girls' High to see where she went to school and past the small green cottage provided by the South African Railways where she used to live. My mother liked Durban because it was English, and deep down she preferred the English to the Afrikaners, in spite of the fact that she married a Boer. In Durban, and in my mother, you could occasionally see traces of the *real* English, of the proper English, because her grandparents came from Scotland and Ireland and England and these people were called things like 'Nan' and 'Nana'. And because the English liked Zulu words, there were people called things like 'Ga', derived from the Zulu word '*gogo*' which means 'old lady'.

And my mother thought real Englishness was best of all, which was why she tried to read her children Beatrix Potter, *Noddy* and *The Famous Five* when we were young and why she looked disappointed when each of us in turn begged her to stop. My mother knew the words to 'God Save the Queen', but not *'Die Stem'*. My mother could name all the Kings and Queens of England from William the Conqueror to Elizabeth II. She knew who cut off whose heads and why. She knew the plot of every Dickens novel and every character in every Austen. She liked taking us to pantomimes even though we found them terribly embarrassing because they made you stand up and *do* things and on one occasion Rachel and I were singled out for not participating and made to sing in front of the whole theatre while we glared at my mother for making us suffer this awful indignity. And my mother knew lots of Zulu words because in Durban all the black people were Zulu including the rickshaw men on the beachfront with their giant headdresses who I thought were marvellous though I was forbidden from riding in a rickshaw because it was 'disgusting for a little boy to be dragged around the beachfront like Lord Muck on Toast'. Those poor sweat-gleaming black men ran themselves into an early grave but I was not to be a part of it. When we were in Durban we ate Chelsea buns and scones, we visited relatives who smelt of mothballs and made knitted Pink Panthers and gollywogs to sell for charity.

The main thing my mother and father had in common was that they both had alcoholic fathers. But my mother's father didn't kill himself; he drank until he had a stroke, which made him a vegetable. Even my mother said that. She said, 'My father was a vegetable for seven years before he died,' and when she said this it made Rachel and me giggle. And because he was an English alcoholic there was a lot of screaming and shouting but no divorce. Whenever she went to Durban she would talk about her father and everyone we met always said to me, 'Your grandfather was a charming man when he was sober. He was *such* a charming man,' so when I imagined him he was always wearing a tuxedo and had a thin pencil moustache because in the olden days that's what charming men looked like. And when we were in Durban my mother would say, 'Gosh, Jack, you remind me of my father. He could be *terribly charming* but he was also an alcoholic. So you'd better watch out.' And this would make me feel very manly because not only did my mother think I was charming, but she thought I was susceptible to alcoholism, which was a very adult disease and very manly indeed. I think my parents used to keep a watchful eye on each other for signs of alcoholism. There were, on occasions, what my mother called 'raised eyebrows' at the third glass of wine or the second double whisky, but this was a sensitive topic. Whoever was doing the eyebrow raising would be well advised to give the matter some serious thought. I learnt as a child that the only thing worse than accusing an alcoholic of alcoholism was accusing the child of an alcoholic. A raised eyebrow could bring about the most ferocious scene, followed by alcohol tipped down the sink, and stormy silence in place of what had been a joyous, tipsy and convivial atmosphere. But these scenes were rare, for in the most part their drinking was modest by South African standards and two glasses of 'green slimy' (a cheap sparkling wine so dubbed by my father) was enough to make my mother light-hearted and the same quantity of whisky would also do for my father. In Durban everyone drank lager all day long because it was so hot, and with the exception of the pantomimes, loathsome affairs, we found all this mixed-up Englishness enchanting, but foreign. My mother, I think, would have loved to live in Durban so that every morning she could rise at dawn and swim in the warm waters of the Indian Ocean. She bloomed in the heat and the humidity while her delicate children wilted and her pale husband roasted.

We walked from the Royal Hotel on Marine Parade to one of the swimming beaches. Next to the car park were the beach toilets. The cold cement floors had little puddles of fresh water. The changing area was busy so I walked into a cubicle and closed the door. As I unrolled my towel to take out my costume, I saw a hole in the cubicle wall. I was surprised that I had not noticed the graffiti on the partition before. The author came to the toilet to look at the boys getting changed and masturbated. He wrote about staring at 'budding young cocks'. The message assumed the reader was in the cubicle for the same purpose: 'As you sit with your dick in your hand . . .' Perhaps there was a procession of people who came to this cubicle to watch boys? Instinct told me that the author was an older man. For my friends and me, homosexuality was a social rather than sexual phenomenon. Homosexuals were boys who were bad at sport and were interested in girlie things like dolls and baking. The author of this message was therefore not a homosexual. He was a paedophile. With the exception of my uncle, paedophiles preyed on young children, irrespective of their sex. They lurked around playgrounds and lured unsuspecting children into cars to touch their penises and vaginas. Even I, with my small, undeveloped penis, would be an object of sexual interest to a paedophile. The fear of paedophiles had taken a firm hold in my school. Many lessons were dedicated to the unique peril they posed. We watched videos with American television presenters. They sang songs: *My body's nobody's body but mine.* The English were as obsessed with paedophiles as the Afrikaners were with communists. We revelled in the hysteria and delighted in the candid talk about sexual organs. For us the world was becoming more colourful and more interesting than we could have imagined. Never before had we considered the playground a potential site for sexual activity. Never before had we considered ourselves objects of sexual desire. I was certain that the teachers were being coy about paedophiles. They were not giving us the full story. It was rude and improper for a stranger to touch your penis but the teachers' gravity seemed disproportionate to the infraction. Surely there were worse things than this. But by now I had learnt that certain opinions were better not voiced. Making light of paedophilia was not unlike siding with the Russians. There were some things that, for reasons unknown to me, adults took very seriously. And I knew that it had a lot to do with saying *someone looked at you funny*, and I knew that saying this was as bad as saying the word 'cunt'. So I knew these things were serious, even if I didn't quite understand why. The graffiti in the cubicle was disturbing. Did I also not stare at the older boys? In scrawling something on a public toilet, the author had committed an act of exhibitionism that frightened me. Before me was the remainder of a sudden eruption of sexual longing that spoke intimately. It was as if someone was sitting beside me and whispering his desires into my ear. It was deeply perverse, so it was important that I masturbated quickly. I stood on my toes as I climaxed and breathed quietly through my nose. As I left the changing room I felt certain that everyone in there knew what I had been doing and I burnt with shame and guilt. To be aroused by the scribbling of a paedophile was disgusting. Surely nobody else on the beach would have done that. How was it that I was capable of corrupting everything that was wholesome? My parents would look at me and think me an innocent child. I rushed into the sea and dived under the waves. I splashed my face. I thought of the brothers with hooks for hands. They were pure. They were too beautiful to submit to these base instincts. I alone took pleasure in what was wrong and it diminished me. And Percy? No, I thought, Percy is like me. I could see it. Percy was sexy and dirty too. Percy wasn't like the hook boys. I longed to be heroic and beautiful but I was ugly and weak and craven. I would stop this. I would stop masturbating because I could no longer control my fantasies. I sat down on the beach with my parents. It was hot and the sun baked my skin dry.

The ice-cream man walked along the beach. His clothes were bleached by the sun and frayed around the edges. Wafts of gas escaped from the styrofoam box packed with dry ice. He dragged his feet in the sand. His skin was grey. Poor blacks had skin like this. Better off blacks could afford to take care of themselves and had shiny skin, like Susie. Every week she bought a large tub of greasy Vaseline. The ice-cream man was weathered from trekking up and down the beach for years. I didn't feel like an ice cream but asked my mother for money so that I could buy a popsicle from the poor black man and repent for what I had done in the toilet.

The onshore wind blew schools of bluebottle jellyfish on to the beach. We could not swim. The stinging strings would wrap around our limbs leaving red itchy welts. We walked along the beach while I poked the translucent blue balloons with a stick. As the wind blew harder it picked up grains of sand and pelted our bodies.

'Let's go to the doughnut restaurant,' my father said. At the doughnut restaurant I would order a Mississippi Swirl which was caked in thick white chocolate so sweet it made the back of my throat itch. The Afrikaners in their beach fortresses remained. Their frugality did not permit such excesses. Why, they were already on holiday with a cooler box stuffed to the brim with wholesome food. What need was there to go to the doughnut restaurant, with its huge fibreglass doughnut covered in multicoloured hundreds and thousands, each the size of a baby's fist?

We sat in one of the restaurant booths and as a special treat my father let me order two doughnuts. When my sister turned away I reached for her doughnut but my mother slapped my hand.

'Did you try and steal my doughnut?' Rachel asked.

'Yes,' my mother said. 'Your brother will *look* like a doughnut if he eats any more.' She looked meaningfully at me. My sister laughed.

'I'm glad I haven't finished my doughnut. Mmmm, my doughnut is delicious,' she said. Rachel could be very stupid. My sister and I went to look at the shops in the street while my parents drank their coffee. I could leave her in an alley until she cried or find a quiet spot to punch her. I looked around. Opposite the restaurant was a group of homeless people. One woman was enormously fat. She lay with her head propped up against the wall and her huge body flowed out of her neck. She had sores that oozed pus and her breathing was laboured. Her hair was patchy and there were bloody scratches on the bald bits of her head. I forgot about punishing my sister and stared at this woman. She looked like a whale that had beached itself in the middle of the city, a whale scratching itself, tearing chunks of flesh from its body as it inched between the buildings and the cars, slumping before the fibreglass doughnut.

'What's wrong with that lady?' my sister asked.

'She's fat,' I said quietly.

'She's got scabs on her head,' Rachel said.

The other homeless people were indifferent and stepped over her. I could not help myself. When my mother was teaching at the Hope School, she took me to sports day and I was completely surrounded by handicapped children. Everywhere I turned there was a new deformity on display in small pairs of shorts and sleeveless t-shirts. I was in ecstasy at this brazen, shameless display of obscene and crippled flesh. There was something alluring about these broken children with missing arms and missing legs. And I wished that, for the afternoon, I might be without a limb too, so that I could be part of this orgy of tragedy, of heartbroken but proud parents, of the paraphernalia, the prosthetic limbs, the wheelchairs, the crutches, like Tiny Tim, the epicentre of sympathy and tragedy and poetry.

A boy, the same age as me, but without his bottom half, lifted himself out of his wheelchair and using his thin arms bounded across the field. His mother chased behind, calling him, like an errant dog. I wanted to chase this half-boy too, but I couldn't, so I sat and watched. There was something charmed about these kids' existence, with their doting parents and earnest teachers. They were a collection of delicate china dolls, singular in their deformity. But there was nothing charming about the whale woman. No one cared for her. I stuck my hand into my pocket. I felt the edge of my purple nylon wallet. In it was ten rand, my money for the holiday. Ten rand was a lot of money. I could buy a model aeroplane or a small Lego set. I was tempted to give this woman the money. I was tempted by the magnificence of the gesture. Ten rand would change this woman's day, her week, possibly her life. I could act like God. And when my mother asked me what I had done with my pocket money, I would say, 'I gave it all to the homeless woman,' and she would say, 'Why did you do that?' and I would say, 'Because she needed it.'

It would be beautiful and my mother would be touched by her son and she would tell everyone this story about how I gave away all my holiday money to the homeless whale woman. Sometimes I was bad. But sometimes I could be like fucking dead Daphne too. I fidgeted with the Velcro flap of my wallet. I inserted my finger between the join of the material and prised it open quietly. I didn't want the woman to hear that I was opening my wallet. I didn't want to commit myself.

'Jack, I think that lady is sick,' my sister said.

My parents had finished drinking their coffee and were busy paying the bill. In a moment they would leave the doughnut restaurant. I only had a few moments to dash and deposit the money in her lap. In her lap? Would I simply throw the money into her lap or would I hold it out to her? Her eyes were closed. What if she didn't see me? What would I say to her? 'Lady, wake up, here is some money for you. Wake up, lady, I want to give you ten rand.'

My parents paid the bill and walked out the door. They stood on the pavement looking at us. My mother said, 'Come on. We're going back to the beach.'

I hesitated for a moment. The whale lady's eyes were open like two evil slits. She was looking at me. As I walked with my parents, I turned back. She was still looking at me. I regretted not doing this one good thing.

* * *

On New Year's Eve we walked to the beachfront where families were letting off fireworks and teenagers were drinking beer and playing in the waves. Some of the blacks were walking down the street shouting 'Happy! Happy!' My mother asked whether I wanted to go on the roller coaster but it didn't have a loop. Besides, there would be little point in going with one's mother. It was the last few hours of 1989. The previous month a wall had fallen in Germany and I, who had always believed myself removed from the masses, different, would have to consider myself anew, for the end of communism erased that sudden and unexpected belch, that ill-considered pledge of allegiance that pealed across the classroom all those years ago: I'm with the Russians. Hundreds of children played in the splash pools on Marine Parade. The water was warm as blood. 'Urine,' my mother said. We didn't know at the time that it would only be a few months until we were all part of the agreeable political kitsch that portrayed a longed-for recon-ciliation finally realised. The great battle was nearly over and the opportunity for feckless young people to do some-thing, to make their mark, to save some blacks, to make some gesture for all to see the inadequacy of our response, was over. Which was lucky really. For at my best, I was a person of very small gestures. We left late the next morning, which made my father irritable. Driving on New Year's Day was a good idea because nobody else would waste a glorious sunny holiday driving back to Johannesburg. My father liked avoiding traffic. By the time we reached the motorway it was already hot and we knew it would be a long journey home. We stopped again at the Wimpy Bar in Harrismith but the beautiful family was not there.

11

Percy and the mermaid submarine

BECAUSE WE'D COME back early Petrus was still away. Swimming wasn't as much fun without him. He'd stand at the deep end and say, 'Let's pretend I'm a mermaid and the swimming pool is my house.' Then he would dive into the pool keeping his legs clasped together, surface in the shallow end, wipe his face and grin. 'Did you see how I can swim like a mermaid? I would love to be a mermaid and live in the water forever. My father says next year he's going to build us a swimming pool. He says all he needs is five blacks and a concrete mixer. I said we must make a picture of a dolphin in the swimming pool with tiles. I even drew a picture. Or a waterfall; a waterfall would be nice too.'

Before he'd gone on holiday, Petrus had persuaded me that it would be good to build a hotel in our back garden. 'If we build a hotel,' he said, 'we can charge people to spend the night in it.' This seemed like a reasonable proposition but I wasn't sure where we were going to get a TV. 'If we're going to build a hotel,' I said, 'it has to have a TV.' Only

hotels with TV were any good. 'If we can't get a TV, I think
we should build a submarine and test it in the swimming
pool.'

'What about a mermaid submarine?' Petrus asked.

'What's a mermaid submarine?'

'It's like a hotel – but for mermaids.'

With some considerable effort, we first stole, then
lugged the building materials for a mermaid submarine
from his father's shed and hid them behind the bamboo
in the back garden. Susie was suspicious.

'Jack! What are you doing?'

'Nothing, Susie.'

'Where you get these things?'

'Oom Frik gave them to us.'

'He give you this thing?'

'Yes, Susie.'

'Your mommy know about this thing?'

'Yes, Susie.'

'Are you making mess?'

'No, Susie.'

'If you make mess I will tell Ruth.'

'Yes, Susie.'

'If you make mess I will hit you!'

'Yes, Susie.'

'You're my baby, I love you. But I will hit you.'

'Yes, Susie.'

It was difficult building a submarine on your own and
I suspected Petrus was more committed to the mermaid
part. I nailed the plastic seat from a stackable chair to a
large wooden plank and dragged it into the deep end of
the swimming pool. For a few moments it looked like my
makeshift cockpit would float, but then the chair detached
from the plank and bits of debris floated to the bottom of

the pool. If I destroyed another Kreepy Krauly I'd be in for a hiding. The previous one had provided hours of amusement when Aaron and Emmanuel pinned Jürgen down and I stuck the industrial suction part on to his crotch. After we'd broken the Kreepy Krauly we tried to repair it with Sellotape but it didn't work so I told my parents that Jürgen had jumped on it.

I gave up on the submarine and my heart wasn't really in the hotel anyway. Most of the time I tortured my younger sister. I dunked her in the swimming pool and locked her in the attic. We played Monopoly and I stole her money or talked her into inadvisable trades. I made her do my chores and paid her with money I had stolen out of my mother's purse. My mother, finally exhausted by the constant bickering and not infrequent floods of tears, sent her off to Julia to spend the day lazing on their couches and using their loos with strict instructions not to comment on the lexicon of her hosts. I spent the morning intermittently masturbating and building a model aeroplane with that sticky and corrosive glue (an inadvisable mingling of hobbies).

I knew something was wrong when, after speaking to someone on the phone, my mother called me and asked me to stay in my bedroom for a while.

'Go back to your room, Jack, and wait there. I'll come and talk to you in a bit.' The evenness in her voice indicated that something horrible had happened. I could see she was shaking a little and looked pale. Probably, I thought, someone was dead. My father? It was not impossible. The sudden death of Jürgen's father had taught me that. Maybe my father had cancer of the spine and had collapsed in his office, slumped over the papers on his desk.

The kitchen door slammed in the wind. I ran to the bath-room, stood on the toilet and peered out of the window. I could see my mother walking with Susie to her cottage at the rear of the property. Susie stumbled and my mother supported her. It is Susie who is grieving, not my mother, I thought, and felt a sense of relief. I ran through the list of Susie's family and weighed the gravity of each death. In the abstract I knew that if it was Percy who had died it would be the worst. I had been told that the death of a child caused a disfiguring grief. My heart raced. I could not bear to think of Susie forever changed. I needed her as she was. Perhaps it was her husband Lebo. Was it bad, too, if your *estranged* husband died? For a moment I felt as if a death had been marked down, determined, and now it was only up to me to decide. Whose passing would cause the least pain? Whose death would leave my world intact? My mother emerged from Susie's cottage. She did not walk back to the house; instead she got into her car and drove off.

I leapt down the stairs to the kitchen and slipped out the back door. Rather than walking on the garden path that ran along the edge of the pool, I crept along the boundary wall, so as not to be seen. A large tree and some shrubs hid part of the cottage from view. I got down on my knees and crawled through the shrubs to the edge of the front door. The sitting-room curtains were slightly parted. I stood up quietly and peered through the window. At first I couldn't see anyone. Then I noticed the coffee table between the settee and the television had been moved. Susie was on her knees. Tears ran down her cheeks and she held her head in her hands. Susie bent over and put her head on the floor. It was a terrible thing to see and I was frightened.

* * *

When my mother told me what had happened I peed in my pants. My mother, not knowing better, held me and said, 'Oh poppet! Oh poppet – don't worry, my little poppet! Don't worry,' and as I started crying she pressed her body tightly against mine and the urine marked her dress.

'It's my fault,' I said. 'It's my fault.'

'Don't be so silly, poppet – it has nothing to do with you. Nothing at all. Stop crying now. Everything is going to be fine, poppet. Everything is going to be fine.' They're going to execute Percy, I thought. They're going to take him to Pretoria Central Prison, feed him a roast chicken, lead him up the fifty-two stairs to the death chamber on Monday morning, read him his death warrant, place a noose over his head, open the trapdoor and break his neck. His body would jiggle and he'd pee and poo in his pants. They would do this with or without Susie in attendance, with or without Susie wailing for mercy. I could never have foreseen an execution of someone I knew; my abhorrence for it stemmed from the improbable possibility of my own demise, so cool and calculated, at the hands of the state.

Percy was in a prison near Kabalazani. When Susie returned home later that night, I didn't even get to say goodbye or that *I was sorry for her loss* or whatever it was one was supposed to say. The house was quiet without her. She had a lot of arrangements to make. I understood there were cattle to be bought and slaughtered; family to attend to. Percy had murdered his father. When Petrus asked why Susie was away, I could not tell him. Petrus would say something crude. He would reduce tragedy to the incorrigible nature of the natives through some expression he had picked up from his parents. And Petrus might say something about how murderers are hanged and that this was good because the Bible said an eye for eye.

Susie returned two weeks later. She had lost weight and looked haggard. She didn't shout at me about anything; she hardly noticed the dirty dishes or the wet towels. Halfway through washing the dishes she would stop and stare for minutes on end before remembering what she was doing and then she would shake her head and say, 'Ai.'

'The ZCC,' Susie had often said, 'they are so strict. They are nice people, but too strict.' ZCC members wore a silver star on a green felt backing to signal their affiliation to the Church and on Sundays they gathered in parks wearing brightly coloured robes to sing and dance. Whenever my friends and I visited fat Thomas we could hear the steady drumbeat sail over the Melville koppies, while his mother told us to 'open our mouths and speak properly' as her husband slunk off into the garden shed. Of course at the time we didn't think there was anything peculiar about the Zionists. That was just the way many blacks worshipped God – and as seriously as the Afrikaners took God, which was very seriously indeed, everyone agreed that nobody took God quite so seriously as the blacks. The ZCC swarmed into every green inch of the city and practised a strange form of pagan Christianity which was enough to make one think the army of invading priests were newly arrived on the colony's shores.

One night, when Percy had returned drunk from a shebeen, he was enraged to discover that Lebo had locked him out. He had pounded on the door and shouted through the windows. His father awoke and told him to leave. Percy was no longer welcome, he said. Susie and I sat in the kitchen as she told me what had happened. I'd made two mugs of tea and put an extra teaspoon of sugar in Susie's tea because I knew that sometimes she liked it that way.

'He was so mad, that one,' Susie said. 'The neighbours say he was drinking. His friends, they are tsotsis all of them. I tell him, they are very bad guys, but he never listen. Why Lebo lock him out? Where he think Percy is going to sleep? He break the door and his father get very angry. His father tell him to go. He say to him he must fok off and never come here again. Percy say his father try to push him out. He say his father hit him in the face. His father is a very strict man, Jack. Too strict, that one. His father hit him in the face and Percy – he get so angry he take the knife and stab him. His own father. He kill his own father. How can he do this thing? I cannot understand this. His father was a nice man. So strict – but he was a nice man.'

I did not know what to say, so I kept quiet. Susie sipped her tea and didn't say anything for a long time.

'This tea is very sweet. How many sugar you put in it, my baby?'

'Two teaspoons.'

'Two teaspoons?'

'Three teaspoons.'

She laughed a little. 'You are so naughty. You! One day you will be *stutla* and the girls won't like you. They will say Jack is too fat. I'm not going to marry such a fat guy. Such a fat man eats too much. I like sweet tea – you too, you like sweet tea – but I don't want to be *stutla*.'

'You're skinny now.'

'Yes. I don't eat anything when I go home. My heart is so sore I can't eat anything. You know this, when your heart is sore you can't sleep. I can't sleep at night. I worry about this thing. You know, Jack, Percy his father was a handsome guy, Jack. You remember? You met him.'

It struck me that I now knew two dead people. I knew one person who had been *murdered*. But my memories of Susie's husband were dim. He'd stayed with us for a few weeks when he was sick so that she could nurse him. He was diagnosed with tuberculosis. My entire family took medicine for weeks afterwards to make sure we didn't get it too. And I watched him whenever he sat outside to make sure he didn't spit anywhere, because we all knew that spitting spreads TB. I decided that if I saw him spit, I would pour pool acid over it to be sure that all the germs were dead. But I never saw him spit, he just coughed and coughed until his face got sweaty.

'You know where I meet him? In Marabastad – in Pretoria. You know Marabastad? We go there to jive. He likes to jive that one. Even me I can jive. When I was a girl I like the music. He like the girls – like Percy. My mother she never like him – she say he's a tsotsi – but my granny – I think my granny she like him. I was so young when I marry that one. I was eighteen years old. He has a big temper that one. Yo yo yo! He used to drink. He liked the beers too much. But then he go to the ZCC. It was good. I like him when he join the Church. He stop drinking. I think he is going to buy my granny a nice tombstone.'

Sammy was nervously eyeing up a large flock of hadadas that had landed in the back garden. The birds, almost the size of turkeys, were eating the leftover bread Susie had just scattered. 'That dog is so stupid,' she said. 'These birds are too big. They will peck his eyes. *Voetsek!*' she called to the dog.

I no longer wanted to talk about Percy and his father. I wanted this thing to be over. I wanted life to return to normal. My mother said it wasn't my fault. She said it very clearly. *Don't be silly – it's not your fault, poppet. It's nobody's fault.* It probably would have happened anyway. It was destined to happen. It was like the parallel universes. In another universe my father was dead because he'd been bitten by a black mamba. And it wasn't anyone's fault – there was no use in blaming anyone about the universe you happened to be stuck in. In *that* universe there was an article about us in *You Magazine* and my mother wore black clothes every day and Percy's father was probably alive, because we would have come home and told Susie what had happened and everyone would have been in mourning and Percy would never have gone drinking because his mother was too upset. And we would have been making all sorts of arrangements, not buying cattle or anything, but buying caskets and arranging funeral services. So there really wasn't any point in talking about it any more. But all Susie could do was talk and reminisce, turn the facts over, consider them anew before putting them back where she found them.

'When Percy get the matric Lebo tell me that he was going to make a big party for him. Invite his friends, make nice food, make some music. He wanted Percy to get the matric. He loved Percy. He thinks like me – his father. He didn't want that Percy is like us. He want him to get the education. He want that he go to the college or the university. Me too I want him to go to university. I say to him I will pay. Percy he's clever, Jack – like you he's very clever. He's not stupid like me. I don't know what happens now.' She fished the tea bag out of her cup with a teaspoon and left it on a saucer.

'We make a big funeral. His family is very angry. They say I must pay. I tell them – yes I will pay. I talk to your daddy to borrow some money. They say it's my fault. They say I am to blame for this thing.' She took off her glasses and wiped her eyes. She cried a little and wiped her nose with the crumpled tissue she now always carried with her. 'They say I am a bad mother. I try, Jack. I want him to get the matric. When I see Percy, he is crying all the time. He say to me – "I am so sorry, Mamma. I am so sorry for this thing."'

The murder stirred something within Lisa. When my parents were out she took Susie aside and tried to talk to her. I think she might even have used her Rorschach cards – even though she could have got into a lot of trouble. Afterwards they were both very angry. My sister slammed the door, got into her car and drove back to Pretoria. Susie slammed the door, walked to her cottage and then came back to the house twenty minutes later.

'Your sister is very cheeky,' she said. 'Your sister is a very, very cheeky girl.' I shrugged. 'Make me some tea, my baby. With three sugars.' I gathered that Lisa had said something about God. She probably said that God was all well and good but that He was no substitute for a *proper* psychiatrist and that church was no substitute for a psychiatric institution. I wasn't sure whether she said this in relation to Susie or Percy but either way Susie thought that whatever my sister had said was unforgivable.

The following week Susie was wearing the silver star with a green felt backing. I couldn't help but stare.

'Yes?' she said. 'What you looking?'

'Nothing,' I said.

'Don't lie. I see you look at this,' she said, touching the silver star.

'No. I was just looking.'

'I joined the ZCC.'

'That's nice.'

'They are nice people, Jack. Every day they pray for me and they pray for Percy.'

'That's good.'

'They say this thing is not my fault. They say Percy is to blame. He make this terrible thing. Not me. But God is love. God will forgive him. You know, Jack, that man from the ZCC he go with me to the prison. He talk to Percy. He say to Percy this thing is over. He must stop crying and he must stay in prison and make it right and God He will forgive him. He say God will forgive anything. Anything, anything, anything. It doesn't matter if it's a small thing or a big thing, God is love. He say to him he must stop this smoking and this drinking and pray to God and then they baptise him. Me too, they are going to baptise me.' She smiled and then laughed. 'I don't like to get into the water, Jack!'

One can't help but wonder, given everything that was happening around us, whether Percy's timing was only fractionally off. Of course we didn't *know* this. It's not as if his father would have stopped being a member of the ZCC or as if Percy would have stopped drinking – but who knew? Perhaps the old man would have eased up a little or Percy, instead of becoming blind with rage, would simply have slumped against the door and slept it off. At the time, I thought that the courts, when it came to badly behaved blacks, would bring the full force of the law to bear on young Percy. It was a blunt instrument devoid of subtlety or compassion. But Percy did not spend more than four months in jail and emerged newly contrite, as was befitting a young murderer from the township granted a second chance. He walked out like the sole survivor of a plane crash, shaken and dusty but unscathed, unable to believe that after this thing, this terrible, life-altering thing, here he was, still alive. It is little wonder he became a devout member of the ZCC. Who else but the Almighty could have interceded so spectacularly on his behalf? I always thought that humanity, not taken individually, but aggregated, their sentiments, their thoughts, their actions, their systems, their judgements, was an ineffective but still functioning ballast against the arbitrary, the random, the absurd, the power lines in the way of the mast, the cancer in the spine and all the other things which were improbable, individually, but still happened an awful lot, when aggregated. But there were men in prison serving longer sentences for burglaries and traffic violations, so one could only conclude that humanity, rather than a ballast against the arbitrary, was, through paperwork and forms and stamps and considered judgements and all that was officialdom, its very agent. There was something amusing in the time it took the universe to make its point to this white kid who lived in a very nice suburb and who had to work really hard to add things to his list of traumas, which still consisted of lost toys and, lower down, dead grannies.

When Percy returned from prison, I watched, from my bedroom, the scrawny young man pull the large metal gates that opened to our house. He was wearing a pair of faded jeans and a grey sweater. Slung over his left shoulder was an old green backpack I had given Susie. The security light in the driveway switched on as Percy closed the gate, blinding him momentarily. He squinted and waited for his eyes to adjust. He looked up. From the driveway he must have made out my silhouette at the window. He was not sure what to do. Tentatively he raised his hand as if to wave. I did not move. Percy put his hand to his head, then scratched his crown. I drew the curtains. Hunched with shame Percy walked to the back of the house. He stayed with Susie for two days, but in that time I didn't see him again. He must have hidden in the cottage.

There was no more talk about obtaining a matriculation. If anything, the terrible events of that night served to confirm everything that Susie believed. Percy would never have killed his father had he matriculated. If Percy had matriculated, he would have got a good job or perhaps even a place at Vista University. He would never have fallen in with the tsotsis. He would never have got drunk. He would never have picked up the knife. Susie was right. A matriculation was the surest testament of a person's good character. A good pass in standard four was evidently not.

'Jack, I'm afraid Susie has decided to move back home,' my mother said.

'For how long?' I asked.

'Forever Jack.'

'But . . . but why?'

'To take care of Percy. This is a terrible thing that's happened and Susie wants to take care of her son.'

'But what about me?' I asked.

'What about you, Jack?'

'I don't want Susie to go. I want Susie to stay here. With us.'

'We all do. We all want Susie to stay. But you can understand why she needs to go.'

'I don't! I don't understand! It's not fair!'

'Jack – calm down!'

'I don't want to calm down. Susie is supposed to live here with us. Susie loves me and she loves Rachel –'

'Jack –'

'And she can visit Percy on the weekends –'

'Now keep quiet.'

209

For a moment neither my mother nor I said anything. The news had floored me. I had never considered, not for a moment, the possibility that Susie would leave us. Susie would stay with my family forever. She would stay with my family until she dropped dead in the kitchen. This was where Susie belonged. You couldn't, it wasn't *right*, to inveigle your way into a family like this and then just leave. That was like divorce. That's why divorce was wrong because it simply wasn't right to wrench people apart without a care in the world.

'You can't let Susie go, Mom.'

'But Jack, it's not up to me.'

'But Mom, what if Percy kills her? What if Percy murders Susie?'

'That's a terrible thing to say, young man. Now I think you should go to your bedroom and think about what you just said –'

'He killed his father – he's a murderer!' I screamed. 'He got drunk and he stabbed him. You said it was an accident but it wasn't an accident. It was murder. Susie told me. He killed him! He killed his own father! And the Bible says an eye for an eye so they should hang him. They should take him to Pretoria and hang him!'

My mother struck me across the face and I started crying.

'You should never hit people in the face!'

'I'm sorry but –'

'You hit me in the face! I hate you. I hate you. You're a . . . you're a bitch and I hate you.'

'Go to your room now!'

'It's all your fault – you sent him away. If you hadn't sent him away it would never have happened. You're a murderer too!'

'Jack – get out of my sight!'

I ran to my room, buried my face in a *Star Wars* pillow and wept like a baby. Then I hurled my toys against the cupboard until I'd broken half my He-Man dolls, but the anger and the guilt and the humiliation and the sadness would not subside. What would I have to do, how much noise would I have to make, before my mother would come up to my room and hold me and tell me that everything was going to be OK, that she was sorry for slapping me across the face, because this was a mean and common thing to do, and that everything would be OK, and that when everything settled down Susie would be back to take care of me? I slammed my cupboard doors repeatedly and waited for the telltale signs of my mother's feet on the stairs. Nothing. If she came slowly up the stairs, it would be to talk quietly and calmly. If she came slowly up the stairs, she might still be cross, but she would still want to talk, she would still want to make me feel better. She'd say, 'Jack, I understand you're very upset – but this behaviour is unacceptable.' I threw my school bag against the wall. I was out of breath and stood quietly, listening. Nothing. If she rushed up the stairs, in a rage, it would be to scream or give me a hiding. But she didn't come at all. It meant she was so angry she didn't even want to speak to me. I sat on my bed exhausted. I sat on my bed for a long time.

'Jack?'

'Yes, Rachel.'

'Can I come in to your room?' I didn't say anything. 'Please can I come in, Jack?' she asked again.

'I suppose.'

She opened the door and slowly stepped into my room.

'Oh no – your He-Mans are broken.' She bent down to pick up one of the broken toys. 'Don't worry, Daddy can fix it. He's got special glue. Daddy can fix anything. But you must be careful cos you can stick your fingers to your face. And then you have to live like that forever. With your fingers stucked.'

'What do you want, Rachel?'

'Nothing.' She sat down on the floor and started collecting bits of toys, trying to work out which pieces went with which torso. 'Mommy says Percy's dad died.'

'Ja.'

'How did he die?'

'It was . . . in an accident.'

'Are they going to put him in a fire too?'

'No. They've already buried him.

'Poor Percy. Is he going to come and stay with us again?'

'No.'

'But who's going to take care of him?'

'Susie will. She's going to take care of him. That's why she's going away.'

'Is Susie not going to live with us any more?'

'No.'

'Is that why you're crying?'

'I'm not crying.'

'You were crying. I saw you.'

'I wasn't crying.'

Rachel picked up one of the broken action figures.

'This one's face looks like a snake. And this one's got stripes. You should call him Stripy.'

'He already has a name.'

'Why is your face so red?'

'Cos Mom slapped me.'

'Did she give you a hiding?'

'No – she slapped me in the face.'

'Do you want me to kiss it better?'

'No, Rachel.'

'Mom gave me a hiding with her tekkie. It was very sore. It was because I wanted to be purple in Hi-Ho-Cherry-O.'

'It was because you screamed like a brat when you couldn't be purple.'

'I'm not a brat.'

'You are a brat.'

'Look,' she said, pulling up her T-shirt. 'It's my new swimming costume. It's got purple bows.'

'That's nice.'

'At school I'm going to put my costume under my uniform. And then when we go to the swimming pool, I'll be first.'

'Good idea.'

'Do you want to come and swim with me? Mom says I'm still not allowed to swim on my own. It's not fair because I'm a good swimmer. Mom says I'm the best swimmer because they drown-proofed me when I was a baby. What's drown-proofed mean?'

'It's when they teach you to float on your back when you're a baby. I used to throw you in the pool all the time when you were a baby.'

Rachel laughed. She got up and sat next to me on the bed.

'Did you really?'

'Yes.

'Like when I was a baby-baby? When I was really, really small?'

'Yes.'

'What happened?'

'Well – I'd pick you up and then I'd say to Mom, "Mom, I'm just testing Rachel again to make sure she's drown-proofed." And then Mom would say, "OK!" and I'd take you by your feet – and I'd swing you round and round my head. And then I'd throw you in the deep end. And then you'd sink to the bottom of the pool and then pop up again – and you put your arms behind your head, like this, and you'd float. And scream.'

'See? I told you I was a good swimmer.'

'No – it's because you were so fat.'

'I'm not fat. Mom didn't drown-proof you. That's because I'm her favourite.'

I laughed and Rachel smiled. It's true, of course, that she was drown-proofed, though not the bit about swinging her by her ankles. And it was true that, as a baby, you could toss her into the pool and she'd pop up like a cork and float, instinctively tucking her chubby arms behind her head, but it was not true that my mother would happily allow me to throw my sister into the pool. She was usually very annoyed when I stole my baby sister and threw her into the pool to show my friends – 'Look,' I'd say, 'she floats,' and my mother would say, 'Jack! She's not a toy.'

'Jack, can I ask you a question?'

'I suppose.'

'Are you going to be a prefect next year?'

'Probably.'

If you had enough friends and got good grades you could be fairly certain of being a prefect. But Susie wouldn't be around to see it. Susie wouldn't be around to say, 'Jack, I am so proud of you. A prefect – I knew you would be a prefect, my baby. I pray to God and say "God, You must make this boy a prefect. He is a good boy, God". And then I give the church fifty cents that you must be a prefect! Jack – you are such a nice handsome guy. A prefect – yo yo yo – you are big boy now.'

'Should we make some cool drink and sit with Susie on the stoep?' Rachel asked.

'OK – but you need to bring me my cool drink. I don't want to talk to Mom.'

The following week Susie went to Kabalazani to live with Percy. Although her dreams for him were over, she hoped, as only Susie could, to rehabilitate him, to return him to civilised society, with the help of the only people she could call on: the Church of Zion. I cried when Susie left. As did my parents and my younger sister. Susie gave us the number of the local payphone.

'If you want to talk to me – call this number. The people they know me. They will fetch me.'

With her severance payment, she paid for her house in Kabalazani to be connected to the electricity grid, repaired the roof and installed a hot-water cylinder. In the back room of her house, she opened a spaza shop, selling cigarettes, matches, paraffin, batteries, cold drinks, sweets, chips and tinned food. She also bought two enormous steel pots. When business was slow at the spaza, she hauled the pots to the local taxi rank and made pap and stew to sell to the passengers waiting patiently in line.

'I'm going to make walkie-talkies. You know walkie-talkies, Jack? You take chicken heads and chicken feets then you deep-fry. Black people love walkie-talkies. Me too, I love them.'

12

It's funny, neh?

MY PARENTS DIDN'T hire anyone to replace Susie for a long time. I'd come home in the afternoons while my mother was still at work and the house would be quiet, as if someone had died. I'd go to my bedroom, pick up my clothes and make my bed. I might make a cup of sweet tea or pour myself a glass of orange juice and sit on Susie's stoep. Sometimes I'd press my face against the windowpane and stare inside the little cottage to see if anything of Susie still remained; a wire coat hanger on the bedroom floor, a tatty poster of Miriam Makeba and one of Thandi Klaasen before the man threw acid in her face. Daddy-long-legs scuttled on the ceiling but kept their distance from the praying mantis larger than my hand, which perched in the corner.

When I was still a toddler, Susie would put the radio on, we'd dance on the stoep and Susie would say, 'Jive, my baby – show me how you jive, ha ha – this one is a player.'

'Look, Susie – I'm jiving!'

'Hahahaha – yes, my baby – you're jiving! Jive! Jive! You jive like Hugh Masakela! You jive like Miriam Makeba! Jive! Jive!'

'Look, Susie – look at me! Look at me, Susie!'

'Yes, my baby – I can see!'

'I'm jiving!'

And the sounds of our jiving would drift across the neighbourhood and Sophie would pop her head over the fence and laugh.

'Say hello to Sophie, Jack.'

'Hello, Sophie – I'm jiving!'

And Sophie would laugh and say, 'Yes – I see, little one.' As Susie shook her not inconsiderable arse and her large breasts, the gardener would put down his spade, clap his hands and call out, 'Yebo! Let's jive!'

'We're jiving, Finyas!'

'Yes, my baby – hahahaha – tell Finyas – we're jiving!' And then Susie would pick me up and squeeze me and say, 'You're so sweet. What will I do without my Jack? My Jack – my little baby. My beautiful baby. You are my son. This one – he is my son.'

If I missed Susie too much, I'd phone the number she left us.

'Hello?'

'Hello. Is Susie there?'

'Who is this?'

'It's Jack. I'm looking for Susie.'

'Susie Mafisa?'

'Yes.' I would then wait while the man spoke in Sotho to people I presumed were milling about the street.

'Susie isn't here – call tomorrow.'

'OK.'

And the next day I would try again.

'Hello?'

'Hello, my name is Jack Viljee. Can I talk to Susie Mafisa please?'

'What?'

'My name is Jack Viljee. Can I talk to Susie Mafisa please?'

'Who is this?'

'Jack. Can you tell Susie it's Jack. I need to talk to her.'

'Susie Mafisa?'

'Yes.'

If I was lucky and someone knew who Susie was and where she was then she would be summoned to the phone.

'Hello?'

'Susie?'

'Jack? What's wrong?'

'Nothing, Susie.'

'You give me big fright. You all right, baby?'

'Yes, Susie.'

'What you want, my baby?'

'I just want to say hello.'

'Ah, you are too sweet.'

'I miss you, Susie.'

'Me too, my baby. My heart is so sore. How's your mommy and your daddy and Rachel?'

'They're fine. They miss you too.'

'And Lisa?'

'Fine.'

'She's clever that one.' And I could hear that she still hadn't forgiven my sister for what she had said. And anyway, I didn't want to talk about Lisa, because I was scared of Lisa and her ink blots. I was scared she would take them out and their power would be too strong. I would be overcome and I would say things and not be able to stop myself and my sister would say, 'Jack! What have you done, Jack? Tell the truth – what have you done? I think you have pathological tendencies.'

219

'Have you got a girlfriend?' Susie asked.

'No.'

'That's right. You are too handsome but you must wait.'

'Susie – please come home.'

'No, Jack. I am home.'

'Please, Susie. Percy can come too. He can stay here.'

'No, Jack. I must stay in Kabalazani. This is my home.'

And I thought I might cry, but I tried to hide it because Susie already thought I was a baby.

'Please, Susie. Please.'

'Jack – I can't. Don't make my heart sore.'

'When will you come to visit?'

'Maybe next month. There is a big party there for the ZCC. I will phone.'

'OK.'

'Don't be sad, Jack. You are a big boy. You don't need your Mama Susie. Are you making a big mess in the house?'

'No.'

'That's good. You are a big boy now. You are a man.'

Susie came to visit one Saturday afternoon. She was wearing her town outfit and carried an umbrella to shield her from the afternoon heat. We all sat in the lounge and drank tea and coffee. Susie told us about Percy. He'd got a job with a builder in the township. 'He's learning how to do the brick-laying. I say to him one day he must do the extension for my house. You too, Ruth and Willem. One day I tell Percy to come here and do you the extension. We make a big room. He goes to the ZCC every day. Every day.' But soon we had run out of things to say. We weren't accustomed to visiting with Susie in the lounge like this. Standing in the kitchen or walking in and out, everyone could talk for hours about the inconsequential things of our daily lives, of who was up to what, about things that had happened the day before and things that were planned for tomorrow, gossip about the neighbours and their servants, but unnaturally transformed, like this, with Susie as our visitor, conversation did not come easily and the murder sat heavily on the strained proceedings. So when Susie said Percy should 'do them an extension', my parents smiled and said this was an excellent idea, but we all knew, and Susie knew, this would never happen, for Percy had committed a murder and things could never be the same again. I walked with Susie to Barry Herzog Avenue where she would catch a taxi back into town. It was the last time I ever saw her.

When Petrus came to visit he asked about Susie. I explained that she'd gone home.

'Oh,' he said. 'Do you miss her?'

'Ja – little bit.'

'Are you going to get a new maid?' I shrugged. 'My mom went to go and get our new maid from my uncle's farm. She said the blacks from the farm are honest. She's very quiet and she can't talk any English. Only a little bit of Afrikaans. My mom says she's not cheeky like Letsatsi and she will never steal from us because her children live on my uncle's farm. She can't run away to Zimbabwe like Letsatsi. Because if she runs away she will have to fetch her children and then my uncle will catch her. She doesn't wear a bra and everywhere she goes barefoot. She showed me she can stick a pin in her feet. My mom says she's a happy black because she's from the bush. They're unhappy when they come to the cities. Black people are meant to live in the bush.' I didn't ask why, if she believed this, she'd dragged the woman to Johannesburg. That year when I was twelve and Petrus was thirteen, our friendship began to fade. We started growing apart when Tannie Vera called my mother and said, 'Petrus would really like Jack to come to the farm with his father. We thought it would be nice because he spends so much time at your house.' I didn't want to go but my mother forced me. It was, as I knew it would be, days of 'Yes, Oom; no, Oom; thank you, Oom; please, Oom' and stodgy Boer food and no television and getting up at five in the morning and going to bed at eight at night.

On the farm Oom Frik made everyone gather behind him, me and Petrus and Anton and all the farm workers, so that he could test his new shotgun and the sound of the blast tore through the veld and it was horrible and then he said, 'Come, we're going hunting.' And I knew that I couldn't do this. So I said, 'No thank you, Oom. I'll just stay at the house and read my comics.'

'But Jack,' Anton said, 'this is why we come to the farm. To go hunting.'

'I don't like guns.'

'Don't worry, Jack – you'll be safe,' said Oom Frik. 'You will be sitting on the bakkie. You don't have to shoot anything if you don't want.' But I wouldn't be moved and eventually Anton was forced to stay at the farm and babysit me.

'You're a sissie,' Petrus said. I wanted to be rude, I wanted to say something awful about how he was the worst *moffie* in the world but I couldn't in front of Oom Frik and Anton so I said nothing and watched as Anton shuffled into the house and Petrus and his dad got in the bakkie, together with two farmhands, and drove off. They returned just before sunset; on the back of the bakkie was the carcass of a kudu. Anton walked to the bakkie and said, '*Jissie* – she's a beauty. Where did you find her?'

'About two or three kilometres beyond the river. There's

that clump of trees by the *koppie* – we just parked under there and waited.'

The animal was still warm to the touch. The blood leaked on to the floor of the bakkie. I stroked its neck which was coarse and waved away some flies that were already settling around the animal's eyes and nostrils. 'But,' he said, 'that's not all.' Oom Frik was beaming. 'Petrus made his first kill.'

I hadn't noticed the clump of grey fur behind the farm-hand, who was already manoeuvring the giant torso of the kudu. Petrus had shot a baboon. He'd shot a baboon in the face. And they had brought it back just to show us. Baboon meat was good for nothing. You wouldn't even feed it to the dogs. It was a terrible thing to shoot a baboon.

Anton was delighted and Petrus blushed. 'Hey, little bull!' Anton said and rubbed his brother's head. 'Who knew you had it in you?'

'He was fantastic,' said Oom Frik, 'cool as cucumber – the baboon didn't even see it coming. He's a fantastic shot – better than you at his age. He's going to be a great hunter.' Everything was forgotten: the National Party sashes and the empty tree house and his obession with mermaids, because Petrus had shot a baboon in the face. I thought I was going to vomit, but I concentrated hard on my bare feet until the nausea passed. Now that Petrus was a real man, nothing could be worse than vomiting like a little girl. I had never seen Petrus that happy or that proud. His father even made us beer shandies by mixing a bottle of Sprite with his Castle lager, which we sipped while sitting around the fire. Even in the dark of the veld I could make out the kudu carcass hanging from the tree. 'We have to get it up quick,' his father had said to me, 'before the meat goes bad. Then your ma and pa won't get any biltong,' and he gave me a wink as if to say that it was all right that

I didn't go hunting. I was a soft English boy and he couldn't expect much of me because I still wheezed when I drank Oros and nothing mattered any more because Petrus had shot a baboon. This was why Oom Frik had brought us here. It didn't matter that I had failed. Petrus had passed. I tried to be happy for Petrus, I tried not to sulk, but I couldn't forget that face, all caved in and bloody. That night Oom Frik and Anton got very drunk and smoked lots of cigarettes. Even Petrus and I felt a bit dizzy after drinking three beer shandies. Oom Frik and Anton went to bed and Petrus and I made a bed on the stoep because it was still hot and Petrus said it would be nice to fall asleep looking at the stars. We lay facing each other.

'Why did you shoot that baboon?' I whispered.

'I had to, Jack. For my dad.'

'I feel bad for the baboon.'

'It's only a baboon. There are millions of them.'

'I suppose,' I said. But I knew that when I told this story to my parents they would be horrified; my father in particular, and he didn't even have to see the baboon's face. And they'd feel bad for sending me.

'Jack,' Petrus said.

'Ja?'

'Do you want me to teach you how to *skommel*?'

'OK,' I said, because I felt alone and I wanted to be friends with Petrus again and I still didn't know what the word meant.

'Lie on your back,' he said, and I turned over. He placed his hand on my stomach and rubbed gently.

'Petrus?'

'Shh. My father will hear you.' He slipped his hand into my pants and pulled out my dick. It felt good. He gave it a few strokes and then I punched him in the face. He held his t-shirt to his nose to staunch the bleeding and then cried himself to sleep. Things would never be the same again. It felt good to have punched him. I punched him for the baboon and for making me come here to the farm. I punched him for calling me a sissie in front of Anton and Oom Frik. And I punched him for trying to turn me into a *moffie*, for doing something to me which felt good. And I thought how Petrus could shoot every baboon from the Cape to Cairo and it wouldn't make the slightest bit of difference. I thought about how I knew this, but Anton and Oom Frik didn't. It would be a while still before they realised that the baboon had been killed for nothing. After that Petrus and I saw less and less of each other, until at high school we said little more than hello when we passed each other on the street. I wondered whether we would have stayed friends if we hadn't gone to the farm, but I didn't think so.

I didn't think about Petrus for a long time until I read an article in a newspaper. During his testimony, a military intelligence officer cited a strange experiment performed on baboon mothers and their infants. (Who knew whether the experiment described ever actually took place? Reading the testimony I thought it improbable, but then I had drawn the same conclusion on the matter of dog eating.) A scientist took it upon himself to prove that indeed everyone does have their limits and so placed a baboon and her newborn baby in a cage. In its base was an electric element that heated the floor gradually. At some point, the baboon dropped the baby and stood on it, to prevent her feet from burning. I thought to myself: the maternal instinct threshold, measured in degrees Fahrenheit per second. The universe had many ways to make you do terrible things. That's why it was cruel of me to punch Petrus in the face.

* * *

My uncle the physicist left the university and moved to the Cape. The demise of his mother and the Afrikaners brought about a kind of madness in him. To fill the years of his retirement he had a number of projects. We were alerted to it when we were sent a copy of a letter from an undertaker in Smithfield. It read:

Dear Professor Viljee

Enclosed please find pictures of your sister's refurbished grave. Unfortunately we were unable to use the marble recovered from the tombstone. To undertake the restoration using new marble would have been prohibitively expensive and as such we have elected to use solid white granite instead. If you are not satisfied, please notify me immediately so that we can come to some other arrangement.

Yours faithfully

Alida van Zyl

There were colour photographs of the grave taken before and after the restoration. My father laid them on the dining-room table with an amused smile.

'Your uncle,' he said, 'is, at considerable personal expense, restoring the graves of dead relatives.'

I picked up the photo of the cracked and yellowing grave. The tombstone read, '*Yvonne Viljee, 1932–1939. Sleep well.*' It was one of the aunts I had never heard about; a dead seven-year-old from before the war; the stuff of fireside ghost stories. The grave was in a state of disrepair and it would have been obvious to anyone who visited the cemetery in Smithfield, if indeed anyone did, that it had not been tended to in decades.

'Do you think he wants me to contribute money?' my father asked.

'I don't know. Are you going to?' I asked.

'Certainly not.'

The new grave, shiny and white, was ostentatious. When I looked at the photo I knew it was something Susie would approve of and I got a lump in my throat. I missed her. 'Yes, this is a nice grave,' she would say. 'Your uncle is a good man. It is so beautiful. You too must make a nice grave for your family.' Then she would enquire about the dead girl – 'Shame, Jack, she was too young. Only seven!' – and discover to her horror that neither my father nor I knew anything beyond the simple facts that anyone could deduce from reading the tombstone.

But the situation with my uncle was certainly laughable. The cranky physicist finding the remains of his dead sisters, gathering up their electrons and protons, shoring them up for, who knew? At least another decade, perhaps a century even? The new granite, this composite stuff, might last a thousand years. The professor would ensure that little mounds of Viljee would remain for the foreseeable future on the outskirts of dreary towns in the Orange Free State and the Cape. Of course, if these shiny new graves needed visitors then he, with his shiny new teeth, would need to do some visiting, for no one else in the family cared sufficiently about Fucking Dead Daphne let alone fucking dead Yvonne who didn't even have an epithet, so thoroughly was her memory extinguished. Though it was funny it was disappointing too. I thought it one more in an accretion of bad choices my uncle had made, beginning with the vote for the Conservative Party who loved executions. How he must have regretted cremating his mother; one less shrine to stake a claim for a dying nation.

Eventually he ran out of dead relatives. He married a pretty younger woman. He grew fat and his ageing joints could soon no longer support his weight, so he spent most of his time in a wheelchair. My parents went down to the Cape to visit him. Much to my mother's dismay he had installed a jacuzzi in his new house. Through the sheer force of his personality he managed to coax my mother into that cesspool of old-man piss and semen. 'It was horrible,' she said. 'He looked like Jabba the Hut. When he got out of the wheelchair, I could see his . . . I could see his . . . ' My mother did not have to finish the sentence. I could imagine my uncle's jelly testicles, bobbing around in that jacuzzi, like poached eggs, and my mother pressing herself in the corner, as far from him as possible, thinking, 'These jacuzzis are even worse than I thought.'

My aunt finally divorced the mad psychiatrist but continued living in the dilapidated house. Her gardener and her maid continued to keep chickens in the backyard. Soon there appeared above her desk a framed photograph of Mandela. That went to show that this woman was a *real* Boer: very expedient.

After they abolished the death penalty my father became a judge. It would have been impossible to be a judge before this. His favourite bit about the job was reviewing the decisions of other courts and it was clear to me that he often found their proceedings wanting. I sat in the courtroom once as a bewildered prisoner, shaking and unsure of what was happening, was dragged into the Supreme Court and deposited in front of the bench. He was two years into a fifteen-year sentence for armed robbery. My father asked the prosecutor some questions and nodded when he spoke. He summed up the facts of the case, the deficiencies of the defence, the inconsistencies of the prosecution and then told the man he was free to go. And the man looked pleased and my father looked pleased, which just went to show that sometimes the random and arbitrary could be a good thing too. He looked at me and smiled and we went for coffee in a crummy mall because the centre of town was no longer what it once was and all the advocates and attorneys had long since moved to Rosebank and Sandton, but the court continued to stand in the centre of Johannesburg and no matter who you were, you still had to come here, to this semi-squalor, for justice. My father was still the long arm of the law, but sometimes it was those long arms that could reach into the machinery of courts and jails and judgements and officialdom, pluck you out and save you, before you were lost forever.

My mother continued to wage war against the principals of her various schools. None of her children used the words fart, bum, fanny, *tottie* or *voël* in front of her. Because boys have penises and girls have vaginas and they use these not to go the lav or the loo, but the toilet or jacuzzi.

On my twelfth birthday, Susie didn't call. She had probably just forgotten. But the next day, just to be sure, I called the payphone in Kabalazani.

'Hello,' I said.

'Hello,' someone replied.

'My name is Jack. Can I speak to Susie?'

'Susie who?'

'Susie Mafisa.'

'Susie is gone.'

'What do you mean?'

'She left. She go somewhere – I don't know. Maybe she's with the Zionists.'

'Don't you know where she went?' I asked.

'Maybe Lesotho. One day she pack her things and she go.'

'What about her house?'

'I don't know. There are other people living there now.'

'You don't have a number?'

'No.'

And because I was only twelve I didn't know what else to ask, so I said, 'OK, thank you,' and put the phone down. That night when my parents came home I told them that I had lost Susie. They told me not to worry. They would sort it out. My father phoned the telephone number and spoke to several people without luck. The people who were living in Susie's house were not there. Later my mother tried. 'Let's give it a couple of days,' my mother said, 'and phone again. She's probably gone to visit some family in Lesotho.' A week later my mother called again and spoke to the people living in Susie's house. 'I'm afraid Susie sold the house. No one seems to be able to tell me where she's gone. But don't worry – Susie will get in touch with us soon, I promise.' But I did worry. Every year there were reports about the accidents on the highways during Easter, as six million converged on Mount Zion, that grassy slope in Natal, to pay their respects to Jesus. I tried to dismiss the thought. If my father's mind settled on the most unflattering, most ignoble explanation for why something was the way it was, then my mind settled on the most horrific, the most gruesome. We heard nothing from Susie. One night, I clambered over the wall into the neighbours' back garden. I was too uncomfortable to ask our neighbours, who we didn't know, if I could speak to Sophie, the old Zulu lady. From outside I could see the flicker of the black-and-white television set in the small servants' quarters. Sophie was making pap on the Primus stove. I knocked.

'Jack,' she said.

'Hello, Sophie.'

'Hello. What you doing here, Jack?'

I wasn't sure how to explain myself.

'I'm trying to find Susie.'

'She's in Kabalazani, Jack.'

'She was. I have this telephone number.' I took out a scrap of paper from my pocket. 'But when we called they said Susie left.'

'She left?'

'Yes. There is someone else living in her house. And when it was my birthday last month Susie didn't call.'

'Maybe she forget,' Sophie said.

'Yes. But I was thinking maybe you know where she is?'

'No, Jack. I don't know.'

'OK – thanks, Sophie.'

'Bye, Jack.'

'Bye, Sophie.'

My chest ached. I was colourless and characterless. I wheezed when I drank juice. I felt every moment of life like a violent assault upon my senses. I was not accustomed to the rawness. I'd lost Susie and I'd never find her again. And I could be pretty sure that I would never see Kabalazani and Susie would never say to her friends, 'You see, this is Jack. I raise him from the time he was this high.' And I could be pretty sure that I would do nothing to give her a nice funeral. And I could be pretty sure that the universe was full of booby traps, but if you were lucky like me, half baked, half formed, you'd stumble through setting them off and still walk out, like the sole survivor of a plane crash, unscathed. There's no accounting for the universe's taste, huh? And in my dreams I saw Susie, wearing a woven hat standing beside a donkey saying, 'You see, Jack, your Mama Susie is a princess. It's funny, neh?'

Acknowledgements

I WOULD LIKE to thank my agent, Ben Mason, who is warm, generous, witty and a delight to work with. I have learnt a great deal from my brilliant editor, Beth Coates, and I am indebted to her for all her insightful feedback and suggestions. I doubt a writer could wish for better. Finally I would like to thank Richard, always my first reader.